HOW TO READ A FOLKTALE

A Merina performer of the highlands. Photo by Lee Haring (1975).

World Oral Literature Series: Volume 4

How to Read a Folktale: The *Ibonia* Epic from Madagascar

Translation and Reader's Guide by

Lee Haring

http://www.openbookpublishers.com

This is the fourth volume in the World Oral Literature Series, published in association with the World Oral Literature Project.
World Oral Literature Series: ISSN: 2050-7933

As with all Open Book Publishers titles, digital material and resources associated with this volume are available from our website at:
http://www.openbookpublishers.com/isbn/9781909254053

ISBN Hardback: 978-1-909254-06-0
ISBN Paperback: 978-1-909254-05-3
ISBN Digital (PDF): 978-1-909254-07-7
ISBN Digital ebook (epub): 978-1-909254-08-4
ISBN Digital ebook (mobi): 978-1-909254-09-1

DOI: 10.11647/OBP.0034

Cover image: *Couple* (Hazomanga?), sculpture in wood and pigment. 17th-late 18th century, Madagascar, Menabe region. The Metropolitan Museum of Art, Purchase, Lila Acheson Wallace, Daniel and Marian Malcolm, and James J. Ross Gifts, 2001 (2001.408). © The Metropolitan Museum of Art. CC-BY-NC-ND licence.

All paper used by Open Book Publishers is SFI (Sustainable Forestry Initiative), and PEFC (Programme for the Endorsement of Forest Certification Schemes) Certified.

Printed in the United Kingdom and United States by Lightning Source for Open Book Publishers, Cambridge, United Kingdom

Contents

Supplementary material

The original versions of many of the texts translated in this volume are provided on the website associated with this volume: http://www.openbookpublishers.com/isbn/9781909254053

Foreword to *Ibonia*

Mark Turin[1]

Two decades after it was first published, a powerful oral epic from Madagascar is once again available to a global readership, in print and online. *How to Read a Folktale: The Ibonia Epic from Madagascar* is the story of a story; a compelling Malagasy tale of love and power, brought to life by Lee Haring.

Throughout this carefully updated text, Haring is our expert guide and witness. He provides helpful historical background and deep exegesis; but he also encourages us to let *Ibonia* stand alone — deserving of attention in its own right — a rich example of epic oral literature. And it is through this exquisite rendering of Malagasy orature that we — the readers — appreciate once again the value of oral literature for making sense of human culture and cognition.

Until someone wrote it down (around 1830), *Ibonia* was communicated only orally. And some 160 years later, Haring transcribed and translated it, introducing the epic in print form to a global audience through Bucknell University Press. Somewhat perversely, while the epic itself remained timeless, the medium of its transmission was endangered. Cultural forms endure and transform, but books simply go out of print.

At an important juncture in the tale, the splendidly named Ratombotombokatsorirangarangarana [Able to Withstand False Accusations] turns to his parents and says: "So long as this tree is green and healthy, I will be all right. If it withers, it means I am in some danger; if it dries up, it means I shall be dead". As for nature, then, so for literature and culture. As long as the *Ibonia* epic remains in circulation and use, whether orally in Madagascar, in print through our committed partners — the Cambridge-based Open Book Publishers — or online in the ever-present cloud, we will be able to celebrate the human creativity that it encapsulates.

1   Mark Turin is the Director of the World Oral Literature Project (http://oralliterature.org/).

Preface

This book is a complete rewriting of an earlier translation, published for scholars in 1994. It owes its existence to the distinguished scholar and critic Ruth Finnegan, who pointed me to Open Book Publishers, and to Alessandra Tosi and Mark Turin, who made the new book possible by their willingness to publish in Open Access. A rewriting was prompted by the discoveries of François Noiret (1993) and his review of the earlier book in *Cahiers de Littérature Orale* (1995). An exhilarating class of highly capable undergraduates at the University of California at Berkeley demonstrated to me that retranslating would be a feasible plan. I am grateful for a second chance to make a rare piece of world literature available to the English-speaking world.

My research in Malagasy folklore began in 1975–1976, when I had the honour of serving the University of Antananarivo (then the University of Madagascar) as Fulbright Senior Lecturer in American Literature and Folklore. University colleagues and librarians and the staff of the American Cultural Center in Antananarivo were unfailingly helpful. Subsequent research in Paris and London was supported by the Research Foundation of the City University of New York and by membership in a summer seminar of the National Endowment for the Humanities. John F. Szwed, who led the seminar, has been a constant inspiration to my thinking. Numerous others have encouraged my work, including Louis Asekoff, David Bellos, Dan Ben-Amos, Jacques Dournes, Marie-Paule Ferry, Melita R. Fogle, Henry Glassie, Alison Jolly, Susan Kus, Frans Lanting, César Rabenoro, Pierre Vérin, Robert Viscusi, and Susan Vorchheimer. Cristina Bacchilega gave very helpful suggestions for the introduction.

This book, like its predecessor, is dedicated to my beloved son Timothy Paul Haring.

1. Introduction: What *Ibonia* is and How to Read it

I introduce to you a longish story containing adventures, self-praise, insults, jokes, heroic challenges, love scenes, and poetry. Here I answer two questions: "What is it?" and "How do I read it?" You might decide it is a love story featuring the hero's search and struggle for a wife, or a wondertale emphasising supernatural belief and prophecy, or a defence of conjugal fidelity, or an agglomeration of psychoanalytic symbols, or a symbolic exposition of the political ideology of a group of people you do not know anything about. You would be right every time.

One way of interpreting *Ibonia*, perhaps a way to begin reading it, is to think of it as a fairy tale. It is fictional. It includes encounters with the supernatural and a diviner who is clairvoyant. It includes magic charms and magic objects. The hero's endurance is tested, and he successfully rescues the princess from his rival. Other elements in *Ibonia* that are common in folktales include magic talismans, which give the hero advice (as birds and animals do in fairy tales): a transformation combat (as in the British folksong "The Two Magicians"), and a set of extraordinary companions (as in Grimm tale no. 134, "The Six Servants"). As in most fairy tales, the time when the action occurs is not specified. Though it does not open with a formula like "Once upon a time", it closes with an etiological tag. And like all folklore, it exists in variant forms. It was read as a fairy tale by its first non-Malagasy readers, who like ourselves could only perceive it in the terms or categories provided to them by their culture. *Ibonia* is more complicated than the tales we grew up with. Below, I take up its non-fairy-tale features and show why it should be called an epic.

DOI: 10.11647/OBP.0034.01

1.1 Madagascar

The world's fourth largest island lies in the Indian Ocean, 260 miles from Mozambique on the East African coast. It was settled by waves of Indonesian emigrants from across the Indian Ocean during the sixth to ninth centuries C. E., at a time when the Swahili civilisation of East Africa was also developing. The convergence of Indonesians and Africans created early Malagasy civilisation, including the language in which *Ibonia* was performed.

2. How to Read *Ibonia*:
Folkloric Restatement

How shall a text so foreign be read, understood, or appreciated? I discovered one path in the library of what was then called the Université de Madagascar, where I was a visiting professor in 1975–1976. On the shelves I found, unexpectedly, quantities of available, published knowledge about Malagasy folklore. The university library and national library held scores of texts, unanalysed, uninterpreted. These called out to me. Faced by so many tales, riddles, proverbs, beliefs, customs, so much folklore to think about, I devised a way of reading the pieces. I decided to read the poems and stories, and even the ethnographic observations on them, as if they were the scripts of plays — as if I could hear them being performed by a living voice. I call this method "folkloric restatement", meaning reading a printed text and imagining it in performance. Others have discovered the method independently. For instance, the Swedish folklorist Ulf Palmenfelt dug into archive material to reconstruct imaginatively an interview between a nineteenth-century researcher and his aged informant. That is the method I suggest to readers of this book. Imagine a performer, an audience, and a social setting: adults and children sitting around under a tree in the evening. That is how folklore is communicated — through performance. History, seen in print, comes to life through folkloric restatement. Maybe it's no more than an intense, self-serving kind of eavesdropping, but how else will we gain any sense of the reality of artistic communication?[2]

Ibonia is one piece among the thousands of items of Madagascar's folklore. A definition of folklore widely accepted today is by Dan Ben-Amos: artistic communication in small groups. That definition prompts the

---

2   You can also listen to a recitation of my earlier translation of *Ibonia* at http://xroads. virginia.edu/~public/Ibonia/frames.html.

DOI: 10.11647/OBP.0034.02

researcher to pay attention to performance. The approach grew out of the work of the linguistic anthropologist Dell Hymes, under the influence of the sociologist Erving Goffman among others. It has been formulated and developed by Richard Bauman. The object of folkloristic study is people's cultural practices studied at close range. Goffman, for instance, studying human interactions closely, saw them as if they were dramas, with characters and prearranged scripts. Folklorists like Barbara Kirshenblatt-Gimblett transposed this model into close observation of the telling of a story; she showed the storyteller and audience to be characters in their own drama, which took place beyond the mere words of the storyteller. This was a new matrix, or "paradigm", for the discipline of folkloristics: performance. Formerly, folktales were studied as texts fixed in writing; now, artists, audiences, and texts were envisioned in a new configuration. Performance folklorists turned upside down the old search for songs and stories as things. Instead of studying texts, they scrutinised moments of social interaction. They stopped trying to explain a particular story as a variant of some hypothetical original. Variation became the norm. What performance theory has to explain is fixity, the absence of variation. Literary studies do not face this problem. *Ibonia* exists in variant forms; one is translated here — one text.

3. What it is: Texts, Plural[3]

What is a "text"? A set of words printed on paper. The text translated here is forty-six pages from a book 6 1/2 by 4 1/4 inches, published in Madagascar in 1877.[4] The pages have sentences that begin with capital letters and end with periods; it has paragraphs. It also has those long Malagasy names, which are more pronounceable than they look.[5] Those long names are constructed out of short elements, each of which means something. Take Andrianampoinimerina, the great king of the Merina ethnic group at the beginning of the nineteenth century. His name is simple: *Andriana* [prince], *am-po* [in the heart] *in* [connecting device], *Imerina,* the name of his land and people (pronounced Mairn'; the last syllable is likely to be inaudible). Thus he was the Prince in the Heart of the Merina. His memory lingers over the story of *Ibonia,* which however is a fictional text, like Homer's *Odyssey* or the Old English *Beowulf.* I call it Text 1; it is translated in this book. Until someone wrote it down (about 1830), *Ibonia* was communicated orally.

How does an oral folktale get to be a text? Someone has to experience the communication that happens when a storyteller performs the piece for an audience, and then write down the words. He or she will probably not record changes in the performer's voice, gestures, audience reactions — only the words. Scholars like Charles L. Briggs, who study this sort of thing, have devised a mighty word for this process: entextualisation. What makes the folklore performance available for study and translation

---

3   This introduction follows a three-part scheme for analyzing folklore, devised by the influential American scholar Alan Dundes (1934–2005), under the title "Texture, Text, and Context".

4   See supplementary material on http://www.openbookpublishers.com/isbn/9781909254053

5   See http://eurotalk.com/us/resources/learn/malagasy.

DOI: 10.11647/OBP.0034.03

is the act of entextualisation. It is worth noting that by entextualising, folklorists mark the folklore performance as a worthy object. The implication is that maybe it is good art, and if it is not, studying the text will tell them why. As to Madagascar, hundreds of folktales and thousands of proverbs, riddles, and folksongs have been recorded, in the Malagasy language, and translated into French and English. University libraries, like that one at the Université de Madagascar, contain these, as well as the great French collections by Charles Renel, André Dandouau, and Émile Birkeli. On the Internet you can find books in English about Madagascar's folklore, by nineteenth-century folklore collectors like James Sibree and W. E. Cousins.

3.1 Who is an Author?

If a poem or story — *Ibonia*, or Cinderella, or The Tarbaby and the Rabbit — is presented as Anonymous, who is the author, or is there one? In 1968, the French critic Roland Barthes said what everybody knew and still knows: "the author still reigns in histories of literature, biographies of writers, interviews, magazines …. The image of literature to be found in ordinary culture is tyrannically centred on the author, his person, his life, his tastes, his passions", as if authors are continually confiding in us (50). In the literary milieu of Paris, where Barthes lived, attention to language had replaced attention to the users of language. The old centreing on the author, said Barthes, had to end. He announced the death of the author. Writing, he said, destroys the very concept of author, or voice. Looking outside Europe, Barthes understood that in non-Western societies "the responsibility for a narrative is never assumed by a person but by a mediator, shaman or reciter …" (49). He was right about Malagasy performers. They conventionally recite opening and closing formulas in their performances, which declare, "I am not the author". Tales, legends, myths were attributed to *ny ntaolo* [the ancients]. One northern storyteller begins, *Nipetraka reo talôha* [The old ones lived there]. *Sôla ny lôhany* [their heads were bald], *Baña ny hiny* [their teeth had fallen out]. These images, which have nothing to do with the story about to be told, are conventional formulas, like "Once upon a time". She uses other formulas to close the story: at the end, she says, *Ke io atany koraña e!* [That's what I wanted to tell you]. *Angano, angano, tsy mavandy fa reo talôha, io volaña e!* [Story, story, not lies but the words of the old ones] (Ramamonjisoa et al. 108, 158). Opening and closing formulas make the storyteller more nearly anonymous. Text 1 of *Ibonia,* as translated here, lacks opening and closing formulas, probably because the transcriber thought of them as belonging to oral performance. For all we know, parts of it may have been sung, as African epics often are, but no singing of it has been recorded.[6]

The "folk" in Madagascar had other reasons for keeping authors invisible. Their tradition required anonymity. The words of the ancestors were preserved and cherished without change. That anonymity is the real-life Malagasy counterpart of Barthes's figurative death of the literary author. At every marriage proposal and every funeral, you would expect to hear the conservative slogan, "We have changed nothing in the customs of the ancestors". The narrator of *Ibonia* was not dead, only anonymous, like the narrators of nine tenths of the world's folktales. The questions do not go away: Who is the author of a piece like this? The transcriber? A translator? A publisher? Does a folktale have an author at all, or is it merely the oral performer's property?

3.2 Texts are Versions

Whether it is oral or written, all literature tends to develop variation. *Hamlet,* Shakespeare's most celebrated play, which has excited and puzzled audiences for four hundred years, exists in several printed versions. These differ enough from one another to present a serious problem to any producer who wants to put it on, yet no one doubts that the version on the stage or in the book is really *Hamlet,* even if the setting is twentieth-century New York City (as it is in Michael Almereyda's film of 2000). Variant forms are produced by poets too. The poet William Butler Yeats, late in his life, irritated literary critics by revising his earlier poems. One of them, "The Sorrow of Love", exists in a manuscript version of 1891, a printed version of 1892, and a final printed version of 1925, all from the poet's own hand (Abrams et al. 2462–2463). Which is the authentic text? The acclaimed short stories by the American writer Raymond Carver were so thoroughly

---

6   African epics can be found in the books by John William Johnson and Stephen Belcher.

worked over by his editor Gordon Lish that readers do not know how to choose between the texts.

Because so much folklore is passed along orally and has to meet the needs of different social settings, folk poems and tales are more obviously variable than written literature. Every new version of Cinderella (there are thousands) has some validity: when anthropologist William Bascom discovered Cinderella in Africa, he helped to establish the distribution of the tale over the world. Folklorists use the terms version for any oral or written performance of a tale, and variant for a version that differs markedly from other versions. But the three versions of "The Sorrow of Love" do not give a norm for comparison, unless you decide that the first one is the authentic one and that Yeats had no right to change it. Arbitrary, no?

If the word *variant* is to mean anything, many versions have to be recorded and compared, to establish a "normal" state from which the variant varies. Nineteenth-century scholars did that. Their rigorous study of folktales assumed that tales are entities that exist "out there" somewhere, waiting for someone to come along and realise them in performance. All Indo-European folktales were then systematically cataloged, by scholars who, in Robert Georges's words, "came to regard stories as cultural artifacts and to conceive of them as surviving or traditional linguistic entities pervaded by meaningful symbols" (313). Those scholars did not know *Ibonia*, but they provide the model for how to read it: as an object existing in variant forms. Being told repeatedly, the story exists in multiple oral performances and printed versions. Texts, I mean. After 1877 it became part of a publishing tradition in which each item draws on the ones before. There is no hard and fast rule for determining which versions of a tale are different enough from the majority of versions to be called variants. Only a comparative study of all versions of the same story will show which variants are significant. Nor is there any hard and fast rule for determining which version is the best, because criteria for excellence vary from one group to another.

IX.
ANGANO NA ARIRA.

IBONIA SY NY FIRAZANANY.

NIHOTRAKOTRAKA, hono, Andriambahoaka atsi-
nanana, fa hamangy an-dRailanitra, ka nitondra ny
zanany : dia Ingarabelahy sy Izatovotsiota, ary Andriam-
bavitoalahy, sy ny vahoakany, —dia Imaroahina sy
Imaromanaiky. Ary naka omby fob lahy sy folo am-
pianahana izy, dia tamin' Itanimaroanio sy Isakatriniba.

Ary dia nihotrakotraka koa Andriambahoaka ava-
ratra, dia nitondra any Imbolahongeza sy Irainingeza.
Ary dia hoy ny fitenin-dRailanitra raibeny: " Ravo aho,
fa tsy holovân-dambo aman' alika ity taniko ity."

Ary dia nihotrakotraka kosa Andriambahoaka andre-
fana ka nitondra any Ipandrafitrandriamanibola sy
Imbolahongeza, ary ny zanany valo vavy.

Ary nihotrakotraka koa Andriambahoaka atsimo,
dia nitondra any Ikabikabilahy sy Ifosalahibehatoka,
ary ny zanany valo vavy.

Dia mba hamangy an-dRailanitra ireo izy ireo, fa
zafiny. Ary dia hamahana azy kosa Railanitra raibeny,
ka dia naka omby ny ombiny, izay atao hoe
Ibetsiviliana sy Itahontaka ; ka dia toy izao no fitenin-
dRailanitra, raha tafahaona tamin' ireo zafiny ireo izy

Fig. 1. Lars Dahle, *Specimens of Malagasy Folk-lore*
(Antananarivo: A. Kingdon, 1877), p. 108.

Text 1, the version of *Ibonia* translated here, is odd — very much a variant
from the norm. It was published in 1877 by a Norwegian missionary,
Lars Dahle, in a collection of tales, poems, riddles, song lyrics, and other
folklore called *Specimens of Malagasy Folk-lore*. There is actually a **Text 0**,
a seventeenth-century document (translated in the Appendix) that is
obviously a prototype of all the later ones, written down long ago by the
first French coloniser. Étienne de Flacourt (1607–1660) attempted to set up
a French colony at the southern end of the great island; his book is the
first grand report on the colony Madagascar would become, long after his

attempt failed. In the story he wrote, the hero Rasoanor vows to capture the wife of a king across the water. His father does not oppose his adultery: the only reason he dissuades him is that the voyage is dangerous. When he returns with the lady, he is received with open arms by his parents. So the theme is the independence of the princely son from his father's wishes, and his parents' final acceptance of that independence. The narrator's portrayal of these arrogant, self-serving people reveals that ordinary audiences were not deceived by the social hierarchy under which they lived.

Text 2 (1877) is a shorter Merina version of the *Ibonia* plot, printed by Dahle probably because he knew how popular the hero was. It came from Vakinankaratra, the region of the plateau south of Antananarivo (around Antsirabe and Betafo, if you want to look at a map). It was quickly translated by Sibree (see Appendix), who was the most enthusiastic folklorist among the British missionaries of the 1870s–1890s. It tells the same story, with a few differences. The hero's aunt comes onstage at the beginning; she and her sister, both pregnant, commit their unborn children to a cross-cousin marriage (that means that if one sister brings forth a boy and the other a girl, the children will marry). Once Ibonia has cut his way out of his mother's womb and grown up, he demonstrates his heroic quality by recovering his stolen dog and vanquishing an adversary, whose subjects accept him as their ruler. On his way home he meets some persons with extraordinary powers, who do not appear in Text 1; they will resuscitate him when Stone Man shoots him dead in the climactic battle. They are familiar characters in other Malagasy tales (Sakalava, Tanala) and in tales like How Six Made Their Way in the World (Grimm no. 71). Two other Merina versions were collected and published by Sibree and Richardson in 1886, in a book they published for the expanding number of literate Malagasy, but primarily for their own circle. Today it is a rare book. Though Dahle mentions a Sihanaka version he might have collected but did not, the geography makes *Ibonia* look more and more like Merina property.

Text 3 (1877), perhaps one of the versions in that obscure little book, was summarised by one of the British missionaries (see Appendix). It shows little of the zealous attention that Text 1 pays to royal families who are disputing supremacy. The beloved here is deformed, yet beautiful enough to attract the hero Bonia. Raivato abducts her and Bonia rescues her, with the aid of three extraordinary companions.

Text 4 (1908) is the lead piece in a revised edition of Dahle's book, edited by a British Quaker missionary, John Sims. His book, *Anganon'ny Ntaolo:*

tantara mampiseho ny fomban-drazana sy ny Finoana sasany nananany [Tales of the Ancients: Stories Composed by, and Customs of, the Ancestors, with Some Beliefs], provides a version, not a variant, by revising Dahle's grammar and spelling. Sims's reedition of Dahle remained continuously in print under his name. That printed book is the only context in which many readers in Madagascar know *Ibonia*. Anyone can buy it from a street vendor in Madagascar's capital city, Antananarivo. The book they know, published by the Lutheran printing house, contains editorial changes far more fundamental and extensive than Sims's. Beginning with the fourth printing (undated), one or more anonymous editors reorganised the book in a way Sims might have hesitated to sign. **Text 5** also appears in that book, which has never been out of print. In 1992 it was translated into French from a 1937 printing, by Louis Molet and Denise Dorian.

Text 6 (1907–1910), see Appendix, is a Merina tale with many of the features of Texts 1 and 2: barrenness, a scene with the board game *fanorona*, abduction of the heroine, a hero who effects his own Caesarean delivery, precocity, a life token, two verbal charms, a house transformed into iron, and a successful combat. In this version, the famous name is awarded to the heroine and the flayed skin belongs to a female donor. It reads as if the narrator was a woman.

3.3 Variants

The meaning of *variant* becomes clearer when we go outside Imerina to look at **Texts 7** (1907–1910) and **8** (1934) (both translated in the Appendix). Obviously, if *Ibonia* originated in Imerina, increasing distance from the point of origin means that versions will be more and more different. These two come from regions to the south, where the people have been carefully studied by anthropologists. The Tanala (whose name means Forest People) live inland from the southeast coast;[7] the Bara (cattle-herders, historically) live farther inland, west of them.[8] Reflecting the less rigid class structure of the two groups, the Tanala and Bara tales bear little resemblance to the Merina tales. The Tanala tale (**Text 7**) has a similar plot to Text 1: the hero is betrothed to his future wife while still in the cradle, she marries another king, and the hero successfully retrieves her in battle with his adversary, aided by magic defences against the soldiers' spears. But consider the

---

7   See http://www.mongabay.com/indigenous_ethnicities/african/Tanala.html
8   See http://www.mongabay.com/indigenous_ethnicities/african/Bara.html

dissimilarities, especially in gender roles. The Tanala hero is less prominent, less assertive than the high-and-mighty Ibonia. The woman he marries as a child is so eager for a husband that after one king rejects her, she is accepted by another, who is less scrupulous about adultery. The Bara tale (**Text 8**) clearly deserves the name of variant. The hero does enter his adversary's village as a disguised flayer, but the abductor is only a sexual rival, not a political enemy, of the hero. Instead of abducting her himself, he employs a vulture to carry her off, and at the end he is stupefied but not killed. Outside the central plateau, then, it is a conventional hero story. The Tanala and Bara stories illustrate what happens when a cultural product migrates from one people to another. The old anthropological term is *diffusion*.[9]

Closer to the epic version, though still far from Imerina, is **Text 9** (1907–1910), a related tale told by the Antankarana (People of the Rocks) of the northeast. Unlike Ibonia, this hero is the younger of two brothers, born after Ranakombe the diviner has aided the childless parents to conceive, by means of an infusion from magic leaves. Once he is born, the hero turns into a trickster: he steals his brother's wife, cheats his way into an inheritance, and kills the rich man who has adopted him by throwing hot stones into his throat. Such ingratitude and antisocial behavior, which would be a regular part of his personality if he were a trickster, have only a limited part in the self-assertions of the Ibonia of Text 1, where transgressions that would be unacceptable from a *hova* [freeman] are tolerated from the hero because he is *andriana* [nobility]. Here as in Text 1, says historian Paul Ottino, "These restricted and limited misdeeds merely herald the excellence of the reign of a civilising sovereign" ("Mythology of the Highlands" 968). Ibonia's antisocial behavior and shows of strength recall the real-life stories told admiringly about Radama II, who reigned Imerina from 1861 to 1863. In childhood, it was said, he was fond of pulling the wings off chickens and setting fire to his playmates (Haring *Malagasy Tale Index* 226–227). These men give a new sense to the old phrase *noblesse oblige*.

The versions and variants of *Ibonia* help to define the two terms. Texts 1, 2, 4, 5, 10, and 13 present *versions* in a chain of editing and publication; they are not variants, whereas texts 7, 8, and 9 conform precisely to the definition of a *variant*, a version significantly departing from the majority of other versions.

---

9   See http://anthro.palomar.edu/tutorials/cglossary.htm.

Text 10 (1939) is an important re-edition and translation of Dahle's text, made in the mid-1930's by a Frenchman, one R. Becker. Knowing something about the French anthropology of his time, Becker made some changes based on Dahle's text, maintaining that Sims should not have divided the tale into chapters, changed the order of paragraphs, or made "corrections" of style. But Becker does the same things, creating other chapters where Dahle made none, and my translation inserts still others. Convinced that the tale originated among the Sakalava people of the northwest (who were traditionally hostile to the Merina), Becker restored some words from Sakalava dialect. He interpreted Dahle's *Ibonia* as a solar myth, in accordance with a kind of mythology no one today would believe (Dorson "Eclipse").

Ibonia's story is still alive in oral tradition. Two Masikoro versions (**Texts 11 and 12**) were recorded as recently as 1978 and 1986. The Masikoro people live in the south of the island, still farther away from Imerina than the Tanala or Bara. They herd cattle; they derive income from raising lima beans, of all things. We may expect them to tell a different story even if the hero's name is the same. Text 11 (Mandihitsy et al. 90–101) is decidedly a variant from all the others. First the hero Boniamanoro reenacts Madagascar's favorite legend: he captures a wife while fishing in the sea. But his father, who is named after the seven-headed monster of other tales, opposes their marriage, as does his other son, Revato. The father abducts the wife, motivating a rather Oedipal quest by the hero to find and slay his father. In the sea he meets three potentially dangerous piscine characters, Big Fish, Sir Shark, and Water Mistress. Fortunately he is able to supply each one with meat, and in gratitude each take turns carrying him part way across the sea. These three moves exemplify a pattern that occurs in many folktales, called the "donor sequence": the hero is tested, he responds appropriately, and he is rewarded with something that will enable him to fulfill his quest.[10] Arrived at his destination, Boniamanoro receives a skin offered by a kind old man, which does not prevent Revato from recognising him in the hoop game. Brother and father are both killed, and the narrator remarks that even a father can be wrong. This text, dominated by the Oedipal theme, brings together motifs found in many other Malagasy folktales. As to the traversal of the sea, realistic references

---

10   Note that the childless queen, at the beginning of Text 1, is tested and receives supernatural aid in conception, as if she too were a hero going through a donor sequence. The text thus awards her equal status to a man.

to maritime voyages seldom occur in those tales, but island people never forget that the sea is near or that foreigners come from it. In folktale, crossing any water can become crossing the sea, and the crossing marks the separation of two worlds, especially when the hero passes over on the backs of sea-creatures. Ibonia, like Radama I in real life, might have conceived a plan to subjugate those from beyond the sea (Ottino *L'étrangère* 464–465), but no such plan shows in Text 11.

Text 12 (1986) is much grander (Mandihitsy et al. 15–75). Again by a Masikoro narrator, it portrays at length a hero, Tsimamangafalahy, "the self-circumcised man", who is intent on avenging his father's death. He is born after an unusual pregnancy; then his father sets out across the sea to challenge a rival king. There he is defeated and slain, thus providing a motive for the future hero, who aggressively effects his own birth, shows his precocious strength, engages in verbal duelling, acquires a magic object to aid his quest, and defeats the son of his father's murderer in a triumphal battle. But in contrast to Ibonia's obsessive quest for his betrothed, which makes marriage the main concern of Text 1, the climactic battle in the Masikoro tale is what all the rest leads up to, much like the gunplay or sword fight in any classic Western or in a Jackie Chan film. Masikoro are a warlike people, says historian Hubert Deschamps, dominated in the past by a "turbulent warrior aristocracy" who were fond of raiding European merchants and ships coming into the southern ports (194). Memories of this aristocracy could provide a real-life model, though hardly an explanation, for this hero's behavior.

Text 13 (1992) is a French re-translation, with erudite commentary, of texts 1 and 10 by François Noiret, today's leading authority on *Ibonia*. It is the basis of this translation, and M. Noiret's translations, notes, and commentaries pervade this book.

Text 14 (1970s): *Ibonia* still lives among the Sakalava, a large and important ethnic group in the northwest of the island. The French anthropologist Suzanne Chazan-Gillig collected a version of the story during fieldwork there. In her own words, with a few parenthetic explanations (translated in the Appendix), she retells the tale from a performance by the chief of the Sakoambe lineage, in the village Andranofotsy. Perhaps some edition of Dahle's book is in the teller's background, but the Sakalava chief reinterprets Ibonia's story to symbolise power relations, whereas Text 1 shows concern over maintaining the royal dynasty. Politically, what is at issue in Rabonia's story is the succession to royal power, which is achieved at the end of the tale. A new form of organisation, which Chazan-Gillig calls the birth of Sakalava identity, comes into being when the aboriginal inhabitants have been subordinated. Normally the elder brother Ravato would inherit the throne; his younger brother's challenge to him, which focuses on possession of the woman Soamananoro, has some of that Oedipal resonance that transpires from Text 11. As Chazan-Gillig points out, Konantitse the diviner lives in the forest and "represents the first groups to settle, who were hunter-gatherers". Destined to be excluded from power by this royal dynasty, they favor Rabonia over Ravato. Two magic objects, the *ody* [charm] and the old man's skin, enable the hero to win the woman and gain the power. Two helper roles are fused, the diviner Konantitse and the old man whose skin is Rabonia's disguise. A potent political symbolism lies in the opposition between earth, into which the combatants sink, and water. "Every time Ravato and Rabonia are overcome, they sink into water, and a well or a marsh appears …. the efficacity of the *ody* is attached to the taboo against lying down near the mouth of a river …. The earth-water opposition makes clear the real content of the assimilation whereby all the social groups in the south, sharing a common history of domination, were incorporated; that assimilation engendered Sakalava identity, at the end of a process whereby the *autochthones* [aboriginal inhabitants] were dispossessed and became slaves …." (164–165). Chazan-Gillig's political interpretation points us to inquire about the theme of power relations in the other texts.

The story evidently was known among Sakalava long ago. Both Sakalava and Merina people speak Malagasy (as all people in the island do), but their dialects are different enough for an editor like Becker to identify Sakalava words in Dahle's Merina text. Since his narrator came from the western part of Imerina, which adjoins Sakalava territory, those Sakalava words in the text should not be too surprising. In former times the two societies were quite different. Sakalava society, "a pastoral society of warriors exchanging slaves and cattle for firearms", contrasted with the top-down-directed Merina society, in which power expanded outwards from the king (Ottino "Myth and History" 243). One historian, Raymond K. Kent, even thinks it may have been the Sakalava who brought guns and gunpowder to the Merina, before Robert Farquhar, the first governor of Mauritius, made his arms treaty with Radama I. Merina society shows plenty of Sakalava influences: "silver chains, funerary dances and chants …, human funerary sacrifices …, the poison ordeal applied to humans rather than animals, …

the idea to 'divinise' living rulers, ... [and] marking the ears of cattle" (Kent 162–163, 241). The *Ibonia* story might have originated among Sakalava, as Becker thought, but the variant forms only demonstrate multiple existence, which is a defining characteristic of any folktale.

Text 15 (1992), the most recent version published, combines traditions from two neighbouring groups, Merina and Betsileo. It was recorded by Noiret, who appends it to his re-edition of Becker and Dahle (Text 13). It shows more influence from the Dahle-Sims collection than the Sakalava tale of Rabonia. Unlike most folktale collectors in Madagascar, Noiret gives the reader background information about his storyteller. This, according to accepted rules for folklore research today, is a requirement of proper field research in folklore. Not only must texts be taken down literally from the lips of informants, but full background information must be given about every informant, and newly collected material must be connected with what has already been published by others (Dorson *American Folklore* 5–6). Noiret passes these tests admirably. His informant, he tells us, lived in the region of Ambohimahasoa. Not every reader will know Imerina's geography well enough to say, "Oh sure, that place".

> The teller, Randrianjaona Julien, born in 1923, comes from an old Merina family originating six generations ago in Rangaina (a territory of the *efa-toko* [authentic] Imerina from before Andrianampoinimerina). Having moved through Ambohitsimanova (Betafo) in Vakinankaratra, five generations ago, the family settled here [Ambohimahasoa] from his grandfather's time, shortly before 1873, since his father was born at Vohiposa the same year as Ranavalona II's visit to Fianarantsoa. Though he prefers to call himself Betsileo, because of language, the [family] tomb, marriages and customs, Randrianjaona preserves a certain number of tales from that old family stock. He likes to recount those evenings in Betsileo country when everyone in turn had to tell a story; from those he enriched his repertoire. His language moreover is a mixture of Merina and Betsileo dialect, in which he is visibly more at ease (238).

Randrianjaona's story is highly recognizable to a reader of Text 1, even in summary. First we meet the heavenly prince (no deity, a mere mortal) with a childless elder son. When his two sons come to visit, he thanks them for their gifts but regrets not having a grandchild. At home, the elder son's wife, instead of weeping, tells her husband to seek a second wife. Barrenness, she knows, is the strongest argument for polygamy. But he refuses, remaining faithful to a barren wife and demonstrating loyalty to his class. He sends her instead to the diviner, who forewarns her that she will bear a *loza ny zaza* [a trouble child]. The diviner's predictions of the future greatness of the unborn child are "signs warning of [the hero's] ascendance", in the words of one of the first scholars to study the patterns in hero stories (Dundes *Study* 142). At his direction, she goes to a standing stone to retrieve the magical *valala* [locust]; the stone stretches high, she captures the childbearing charm, and she takes it back to the diviner to grill it. As in Text 1, her victory over stone (mineral) and *valala* (animal) establish her supremacy over the subordinate realms. As soon as it is cooked, the magic *valala* impregnates her by being swallowed. Startling images of this kind are typical of hero tales. Lord Raglan, a crusty British aristocrat who analysed such tales in his book *The Hero*, pointed out that again and again, "the circumstances of his conception are unusual" (174). During her pregnancy, the hero takes his name, speaks, and betrothes himself to Iampelasoamananoro, Girl of Grace, wife of the famous *ombiasy* [diviner] Rainivato (Rock). After six years he tells her to swallow a knife in a banana and he will cut his way out, thus getting born and circumcised at the same time. Randrianjaona, the narrator, remarks that the mother does not die in childbirth.

There is much more to Randrianjaona's wideranging story. Growing up as in Text 1, the hero shows his kingly qualities, which are again rather antisocial: he beats his playmates in sports and upsets women's water-jugs. His father attempts to do away with him but is unsuccessful (Raglan 174: "At birth, an attempt is made, usually by his father ..., to kill him"). His mother sends him to fight a *voay* [crocodile]; he sets out, telling his companions to watch for blood in the stream. If the crocodile wins, the visible blood will be Ibonia's, but if Ibonia wins, the current will carry its body away and its blood will appear downstream. The hero's victory over the crocodile foreshadows his victory over his adversary. Disguised in an old man's skin, he passes himself off as a slave of a previous generation. When he wins at *fanorona* (another forecast of victory), the suspicious Rainivato wants to kill him but is prevented by his father ("Are you mad, to kill a slave of my ancestors?"). In the fields, he thinks to trap him under the hooves of the cattle, but they do not touch him. Iampelasoamananoro recognises him ("It's you!") and agrees to go home with him; standing at the window, she watches him wrestle and beat Rainivato into the ground. The successful victory of the hero over his adversary corresponds to Raglan's point 11, victory over a king (175), and incorporates the worldwide combat myth into the story. The father allows him to take her home. "That is why marriage is a serious thing", says the narrator. "When you say wife, that means wife. That's why marriage is a serious thing. So they say, tandremo ny malaka vadin'olona, Beware of taking another man's wife. That is the story of Ibonia" (Noiret 238–267). Wife-stealing is the luxury of a few privileged Merina families. The narrator's concluding words echo what Ibonia says at the end of Text 1. More distantly they echo the edicts about marriage of the real-life king Andrianampoinimerina, two centuries ago. These edicts, well known to a royal audience, are a climactic episode in the definitive history of Merina royalty, the *Tantaran'ny Andriana* [Royal Histories]. Resemblances between this Betsileo-Merina Text 15 and Text 1 point to an unbroken chain of oral and written tradition.

3.4 Variability = Authenticity

Oral and written traditions exist side by side everywhere in the world. How can we declare that a particular text is only oral? The desire to authenticate oral texts, to imagine an "original" that is free from possible written influence, has motivated many folklorists. It is still a popular notion for many people. Authenticity, for the collector in Dahle's time, would be present in a collected text if three conditions were met. (1) The tale would have to have been invented in a remote time by ancestors of the informant, or members of some related tribe; (2) the tale would have to have been learnt by the informant by means of an unbroken chain of oral transmission since that invention; (3) European influence would have to be proved to be absent. One who got caught in this dilemma was probably the most insightful *malgachisant* (scholar of Malagasy language and culture) of that time, Gabriel Ferrand (1864–1935). He found such close parallels between two tale texts he collected and two fables by France's classic author Jean de La Fontaine (1621–1695) that he wondered about a connection. A Malagasy translation of La Fontaine, he knew, had been published in the 1830s and reprinted in 1867 and 1875, as part of France's never-ending programme of cultural colonisation. The scrupulous Ferrand had to convince himself that the informant could not have been influenced by that book. Hard to believe: resemblances so detailed, in a structure so complex, could not have arisen except by diffusion. The same issue today is delicately handled by Noiret, analysing Text 15. Could it, he asks, be the present-day descendant of a distinct oral tradition, untouched by the popular Dahle-Sims collection? Are the assertions that Randrianjaona heard the story as a child enough to "decontaminate" his version? Or is Text 15 simply a folktale, reinterpreted according to Betsileo cultural emphases? Noiret finds a crucial hint in the hero's name. Randrianjaona insisted in performance that it had to be accented on the last syllable — ee-boo-NYAH. That accenting might indicate Arabic origin, or it might be merely a mispronunciation in the printed versions (Noiret 239–240). The search for authenticity will never stop, as Regina Bendix has definitively shown, but it remains true that folklore may be oral or written, and that Noiret's text exists in the context of the other versions and variants (see appendix). The variability of *Ibonia* — which means its persistence in tradition, therefore its popularity — is what constitutes its authenticity.

4. Texture and Structure: How it is Made

Texture asks about the presented surface of a work — its words, sounds, images; its component parts; its style. Structure asks how the parts fit together to create a whole. Texture and style in *Ibonia* are certainly mixed. If you read Dahle's printed text carefully, you see rhythmic, measured lines; the narrator is relying on these to move the story ahead.

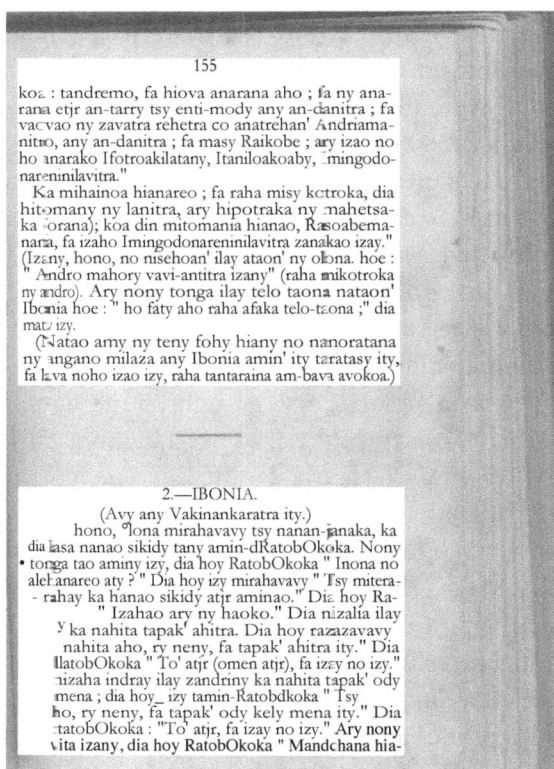

Fig. 2 Lars Dahle, *Specimens of Malagasy Folk-lore*
(Antananarivo: A. Kingdon, 1877), p. 155.

DOI: 10.11647/OBP.0034.04

In dialogue he includes even more rhythm and measure, coming closer to verse. Towards the end he switches into the kind of prose other Malagasy narrators use for folktales. The mixing of styles, which shows in the translation, was the first thing the enthusiastic Sibree noticed about it. The tale, he said,

> includes a great number of incidents not contained in either of the foregoing [versions, i.e. Texts 2 and 3], and a good deal more of the miraculous. In this variant a locust comes out of the fire, settles on the head of Ibonia's mother, sinks into her body, and so becomes the origin of the wonderful child. A long conversation is held between the child and its mother before its birth as to where he should be brought forth, a great number of places being proposed, but successively rejected for various reasons, until at length he is born while his mother sits in a golden chair of immense size. Wonderful portents accompany his birth; for he announces that he is "God upon earth", and that a thousand canoes could not bear him over the water, &c. All living things are broken, the rocks and the heavens resound, the earth turns upside down and this, they say, was the origin of earthquakes. ("Malagasy Folk-Tales" 57)

No doubt these incidents do retard the narrative, if James Sibree was looking for linear movement. They could be called digressions. So could the prologue in heaven, the scenes of self-praise and of mutual boasting between hero and adversary, and so on. The editor Becker rejected some of these scenes as inauthentic, verbose, confused in style, rhetorical jugglery in doubtful taste. Therefore, by his logic, they had to be later oratorical interpolations. Such things do not occur in the Grimms' *Kinder- und Hausmärchen*. But notice: by classifying some parts as digressions or interpolations, Sibree and Becker were imposing their own aesthetic categories, assuming, indeed prescribing, that a folktale should move directly from point to point. They brought European categories and expectations to this strange product of a mixed Indonesian-Indian-African culture, while Text 1 was enacting a different aesthetic, expanding the narrative. This it does by inserting, framing in, other genres.

Framing, for a major part of human history, has been the storyteller's principal means of expanding an oral tale. Embedding one plot in another is the most familiar form of framing. Homer does it when Odysseus recounts his adventures on the way to Calypso's island. As everybody knows, the *Arabian Nights* consists of several dozen plots, framed into one — Shahrazad's successful attempt to preserve her own life by performing stories. Those books, Chaucer's Canterbury Tales, and Boccaccio's Decameron, all use this device. All are tales about storytelling.

Framing tends to reflect its social context. It is a favorite device of narrators in complex societies like Imerina, where control is exerted from the top down. During the two centuries before Dahle recorded *Ibonia*, Imerina was undergoing what is now called vertical integration, at the hands of the successive sovereigns, Andrianampoinimerina, Radama I, and Ranavalona I. The construction of *Ibonia*, with its insertion of other poetic genres, is a microcosm of vertical integration. In Imerina, as well as in societies far removed, framing is the device that makes possible, at least for the narrator of Text 1, the large, inclusive genre called epic. The narrative cycles of both Ireland and India drop in stories about events related only distantly to the main story. Sometimes the only connection is the appearance of a certain character. Analytically, to interpolate an event looks like a way of expanding the short forms of folk literature, to solve the problem, "How shall a long piece be constructed?" The genres available to a nineteenth-century Merina storyteller range from small to large. Text 1 of *Ibonia* is remarkable for the number of styles and genres it comprises.

4.1 Genres: Proverbs, Riddles, *Hainteny*, Panegyric, Verbal Duelling

The smallest genre of verbal art that a narrator can quote is the one-sentence aphorism or proverb. Interpolations in African epic can be far briefer than what we find in *Ibonia*. In the Nyanga epic of central Africa, observes the collector-translator Daniel Biebuyck, the narrative is repeatedly interrupted by "aphoristic statements and terse formulations which, with their highly condensed thought, are difficult to translate" (*Hero and Chief* 6). Perhaps at those points the narrator is quoting a known sentence, or else he is creating one on a traditional model. That is known to be the favorite device of Malagasy orators, to show reverence for the words of the ancestors by sounding like them (Haring *Verbal Arts* 141–146). *Ibonia* contains few one-liners. One is "That is how earthquakes first appeared", which is an "etiological tag", a pseudo-explanation for something everybody knows. Etiological tags in *Ibonia* concern the origin of earthquakes, of sea waves, and of the expression "a bad day for old women" as something to say when thunder is heard. They depart from the narrative to take the hearer momentarily back to the real world. Aphorisms in *Ibonia* are few.

Riddles: Normally, riddling is a competitive game played by children. You win if you know the answer; if you do not, and have to learn the right answer from the questioner, you have learned something about the way adults use metaphor. In riddles like "White chicks filling a hole. — Teeth in the mouth", or "My grandmother's ox bellows day and night. — A waterfall", the important information is hidden. Important information always should be hidden, according to Merina custom (Haring "Malagasy Riddling" 166). Riddles are a prime tool of learning about how language works, so it is not surprising that baby Ibonia likes the ridgebeam of the house as a possible birthplace, "because of the thousand men suspended and the three men separated". Only those in the know, like the Merina audience or an outside expert, can interpret the metaphor. The thousand men awaiting command are the rafters (the word for them, *rozaroza*, also means penis). The three standing men are a phallic symbol of authority. Unborn baby Ibonia uses riddle language again when he rejects water for his birth: "it is a big mat that cannot be rolled up, a lamba that cannot be folded, a pillow that cannot be carried." Each time, the second term contradicts the first, a very frequent device for riddles. Allusiveness of this kind expresses a Malagasy fondness for indirectness.

Hainteny: The great refinement of metaphor, in Merina poetic discourse, is a genre European readers do not know: the traditional poetic form *hainteny*. The word means "word play" or "beautiful language", though a more accurate translation is "the art of the word". It is a sort of verbal table tennis or duel. One etymology connects *hainteny* with its homonym *ainteny*, breath of the word or life of words. "In traditional poetry", writes the great authority on the genre, Bakoly Domenichini-Ramiaramanana, "the word is simultaneously animated and dominated by inspiration, by the breath. Breathing determines both the measure and the melodic line of the verses, just as their rhythm often creates balance, parallelism, and symmetry" (103–106). This etymology marks the genre as poetic. In its name and nature, the *hainteny* relies on the same functions as all African poetic language — ambiguity (double meaning) and simultaneous plural meanings. Paul Ottino, who had the deepest understanding of Madagascar's culture, connected these functions to history — the people's Malayo-Polynesian background. In highland Madagascar, Ottino says, verbal artistry expresses a maximum of thought with a minimum of words, makes constant allusions to proverbs and folktales, and relies continually on metaphor for the sake of dissimulation or obscuring another meaning ("Un procédé littéraire"). In this poetry, brief allusions continually refer to something external to the words. That is, the words point to a symbolic significance behind their manifest meaning, which the audience is expected to recognise. Allusiveness is coupled with ambiguity. The terms of a verbal message can possess several different, or even opposed, semantic values. Before World War I, the French literary man Jean Paulhan (1884–1968) collected and translated a large number of these oral poems. He noted that they were performed as a verbal duel, like riddling: each text calls for a "comeback", called setriny. Sometimes, Domenichini-Ramiaramanana observes, they were chanted in a style known as "falling rice", vary raraka. Inserted into a hero tale, they are a structural equivalent to oral formulas, which Albert Lord showed to be essential to the composition and performance of Homeric epic.

Hainteny poems are dialogues. The performers continually rely on a question-and-answer form, in which the second part of the text balances or caps the first. Here is a brief example from Paulhan. A man speaks and a woman answers.

> "I am an ant.
> They say off there to the west
> are ricefields with small, small rice".
>
> "It's not the ricefields
> whose rice is small, small.
> It's the love of us two
> that is small, small".   (*Les hain-tenys* 214)

The two speakers are debating about the most accurate use of metaphor, as their means of discussing their love affair. It is a poem about poetry. Leonard Fox definitively collects the largest number of these haunting poems in his book of translations. He likens this one to the Japanese *haiku* (413 n.100). Another *hainteny* is a dialogue between our hero, Iboniamasiboniamanoro (he of the clear and captivating glance), who does not forget to praise himself, and a rejected woman who tells him,

> *ny fitia efa ho lany*
> *sy ny fitia efa hinahaka*
> *tsy mba itohizam-pangoka intsony*
> The love that will soon be exhausted
> and the love that will soon be dispersed —
> its broken threads can never be united. (216–217)

Panegyric and verbal duelling: *Hainteny* most often appear in *Ibonia* when the hero or his adversary praises himself. In Imerina, many traditional *hainteny* include praise, sometimes reciprocal.

Rafaralahy said:
  "Are you Andrianaivo of Namehana?
  When he stands erect, he eats *aviavy* fruit,
  when he bends down, he eats *amontana* fruit;
  in the evening, he plays with limes,
  and in the morning he makes lemons roll".
  "Yes, I am he",
  he said in reply.
  "Are you Rafaralahy, the son of those in Iarivo?
  If he is poor, he places money in his mouth,
  if he is rich, he is not sued for debt;
  if he rides an animal, he is not slandered,
  and if he swings on a palm, he is not reproached".
  "Yes, I am he",
  he answered. (Fox 322–325)

Reciprocal dispraise — insult, in other words — was a normal poetic genre in Imerina: a verbal duel. I wonder if it still is in use. One tale of mutual insult between the fly and the ant looks much like a *hainteny*-like rhetorical display (Richardson, "More Folk-lore" 452–456). A mutual-insult story, which Dahle collected (303) and Sibree translated ("The Oratory" 316), pits the chameleon (so much prized today by conservationists concerned about Madagascar's wildlife) against the lizard. When chameleon remarks, "Life is full of danger", lizard replies, "You think so because you're so thin, with your bulging eyes". "As for you", says chameleon, "you think like that because you're ugly and dirty brown". Reciprocal insult is a dramatised, metaphorical form of another folklore genre, the ethnic slur or ethnic insult.[11] Both insult and praise are crucial to the magnitude and inclusiveness of *Ibonia*, which derives its force as metaphor from the stature and exploits of the hero. Praise and insult raise the hero and his antagonist to a stature larger than life. Neither panegyric nor verbal duelling is a mere rhetorical flourish interrupting the narrative; it motivates the whole story. Laudatory names are given to Stone Man, always by women. Living-Lady, Ibonia's aunt, calls Stone Man a meteor and a thunderbolt, and his mother echoes these praises later: "His fingers are horns; he makes hammers of his fists; his head he uses as an anvil". Ibonia's betrothed, the Girl of Grace, calls him "a disaster man, a calamity man, a thorn it's better not to touch".

---

11 Ethnic slurs usually attribute certain characteristics to social groups; in effect, they constitute a popular account of the national character of other tribes or nations, generally in very uncomplimentary terms.

He also praises himself in a *hainteny*:

> I am not stopped by a thousand pirogues.
>> Those who ford I gnaw up their loins,
>>> those who cross, I kill by thousands.

Ibonia is willing to concede to Stone Man the names Nothing-Man-Who-Is-Seeking-Trouble, Owner-of-Big-Lands, and Owner-of-Wide-Lands. An adversary has to be genuinely formidable; think of Grendel in *Beowulf* or Satan in *Paradise Lost*.

The praises given to the hero's antagonist, however, are secondary to the praises given to Ibonia himself. These are no mere literary convention. They take their style from the widespread Malagasy and African practice of changing one's name at different stages of life (Ruud 171–180, Kottak 217–222). When his mother tries to name him, he hears and rejects four honourific names. While his mother is in labour, he pours forth an extended passage of self-praise in *hainteny:*

> I am an edible arum in the chink of a rock
>> uncrushed by any foot
>>> its leaves not eaten.

Self-praise of this sort is a frequent theme of *hainteny*, drawn from his stock of fixed phrases, seldom made up by the performer. To show Ibonia as a *hainteny* speaker is to claim for him the oratorical skill of an elder.

Clearly, not all of the tale is poetry. Some interpolated incidents are ordinary, independent folktales with a heroic tinge. In one frequent scene, a hero or heroine returns in disguise and is seen reflected in a pool (Haring *Malagasy Tale Index* 193–196, 202–203, 363–371, 411–412, 474–475). Ibonia reenacts this familiar incident. Moreover, the scenes in which Ibonia begins to be recognised by his skill at playing *fanorona*, throwing cross-sticks, or bullfighting have analogues in the Malagasy repertoire: there are several Malagasy versions of the international tale The Youth Who Wanted to Learn What Fear Is (Grimm no. 4), in which the hero reveals his superior qualities. These blocks of independent material, probably performed without much heightening of voice or gesture, are interludes framed into the epic to contrast with the panegyric and verbal duelling.

If we compare Text 1 to the other versions of this tale in the appendix, it is clear that the narrator conceives its style as embracing all these genres, which he knew were performed independently, and bringing them into one structure. A European forerunner of this practice was "the

Italian epic poet Torquato Tasso [,who] sought such unity-in-diversity in his massive romantic epic *Jerusalem Delivered* (first complete edition, 1581)" and who was one model for John Milton's conception of epic in *Paradise Lost* (1667) (Flannagan 298). It is these parallels that justify calling *Ibonia* an epic.

4.2 Riddle language, metaphor, metonymy

The three genres inserted into the epic rely on indirect, figurative poetic language, which is used all over the African continent and the Indian Ocean islands. Riddles, *hainteny*, and verbal duelling illustrate "riddle language". This is Geneviève Calame-Griaule's term for an African way of speaking whereby a speaker both hides and reveals his thought. You attempt to communicate, but indirectly; you practice verbal ambiguity so as not to undo social cohesiveness. African-American folklore and literature use riddle language in the form of "signifying", speaking indirectly and ironically, knowing that the target is present and will hear. Signifying is masterfully captured by Zora Neale Hurston in her classic *Mules and Men*. A compelling theory of African-American literary criticism by Henry Louis Gates is built on signifying. Folktales from the slavery era in the United States and the colonial era in Madagascar are riddle language in narrative form, always referring to something beyond the literal. The two-sided game *fanorona*, which Ibonia plays twice, is a nonverbal model for the verbal genres. It is as metaphorical as they are.

    Metaphor and **metonymy** are key terms of analysis for a work like *Ibonia*. Beginning from the work of a great linguist, Roman Jakobson (1896–1982), critics and researchers have deepened our understanding of metaphor and metonymy. Topics in language, Jakobson found, may be connected through being either similar (alike) or contiguous (in contact with each other). Later brain research places metaphor and metonymy at the centre of human intelligence. Researchers like George Lakoff are finding that they are not mere decorative figures of speech, as the handbooks of literary terms say, but are a matter of thought; that metaphorical language is a normal, everyday part of the way human beings speak and talk (123–124). To express similarity in condensed fashion, we use metaphor. Poetry often applies a word denoting one thing or action to something seemingly different. In this *hainteny* (collected by Jean Paulhan) a man's first wife speaks:

Kotsakotsa rambon-damba
  Rano saiky nosotroiko
    Notsipitsipiaan'ilay sahona

The fringe of my shawl is damp
  into the water I was about to drink
        a frog jumped
(*Les hain-teny merinas* 230–231)

Her shawl (lamba) is damp because she has been drying her tears with it. Yet she denies having wept; the frog symbolises the young second wife, for whom her husband is neglecting her. About a Chinese poem, in which a wife speaks in similar mood, Ezra Pound observed, "The poem is especially prized because she utters no direct reproach" (55). The indirectness of metaphor is a help for handling such delicate matters. Cultures like the Merina develop metaphor from their normal way of speaking into a refined literary diction.

Metonymy, the other term Jakobson expounded, is a figure of speech in which the literal name for something is applied to something it is closely associated with. It expresses contiguity. The textbook example for British people is "Whitehall", meaning the office or authority of government. A Malagasy reader might say, "I have read all of Jean-Joseph Rabearivelo", using the name of Madagascar's most eminent poet (1901–1937) to mean his books of poetry. Metaphor and metonymy are at the base of all the "minor genres" of Malagasy folklore — riddles, *hainteny*, and verbal duelling — which are inserted into the story. They transform the hero tale we see in Texts 2–6 into an epic. Any hero's story is a complex metaphor affording an opportunity to fantasise a powerful and successful life.

The texture of *Ibonia* can also be seen from a different angle, as an assemblage of parts on a pre-existing skeleton.

4.3 Motifs

A large structure like *Ibonia* is made up not only of other folklore genres, but, more microscopically, of particles, which folklorists call motifs. The characters, incidents, and objects in any tale are distinct enough to be visible, though they are usually too small to constitute a whole story. Folkloristics used to depend on the study of motifs, and the larger units called tale types, on the assumption that a traditional folktale is composed of characters, incidents, and objects, arranged into recurrent, recognizable sequences. That atomistic view is defined in a fundamental tool of the folklorist, Stith Thompson's *Motif-Index of Folk Literature*. It is a classification of the molecules of narratives, as if to say, "All folktales, ballads, myths, fables, mediaeval romances, *exempla, fabliaux,* jest-books, and local legends are made of one matter common to them all, and here's the alphabetical catalogue of it". The *Motif-Index* is not only a dictionary of familiar quotations, but also an encyclopedia of world imagery. When you glance through it, you think, "Surely everything that there is can be described by one of Thompson's motifs, with its letters and numbers". If something new is invented, a new motif can be invented to peg it. As an empirical tool, the motif concept aims at identifying the component parts in a body of collected stories. Since a motif may occur in many different stories, which may or may not be historically related (think of a princess being abducted by a monster), it enables comparison with other (especially European) repertoires. The *Motif-Index* is a monument of the comparatism that makes folkloristics a discipline.

Thompson's *Motif-Index* proves useful for discovering component elements of *Ibonia*. Thompson set up, labeled, and numbered three large categories: actor motifs, object motifs and incident motifs. Actor motifs refer to the characters found in a story: D1712, Soothsayer (diviner), or K2221, Treacherous rival lover. Object motifs refer to special objects that figure in it: D482, Stretching objects, or E781, Life token. Incident motifs give labels and numbers to particular incidents that are important in the story, for example A511.1.2, Culture hero speaks before birth, or H41.5, Unknown prince shows his kingly qualities in dealing with his playmates. Folktale scholars normally try to list the motifs in their texts (see appendix), especially as a means of connecting newly collected material with what is already known.

Here are some of the motifs found in *Ibonia*, in the order in which they appear. Thompson's catalog wording sometimes seems irrelevant to a particular narrative, but that is a consequence of any classifying process. A210, Sky-god, A211, God of heaven. Z71.2.1, Formula: north, south, east, west. "The very idea of a 'Prince of the centre of the Earth'", Ottino writes, "involves a symbolism of space that is itself inseparable from a political intention: to found a dynasty outside of the common order, the necessary prerequisite for sovereignty on earth" ("Mythology of the Highlands" 965). A500, Demigods and culture heroes. D1712, Soothsayer (diviner); D1810.0.2,

Magic knowledge of magician. M311, Prophecy: future greatness of unborn child; perhaps M343, Parricide prophecy. F790, Extraordinary sky and weather phenomena. D482, Stretching objects. K1837, Disguise of woman in man's clothes. D931, Magic rock; D1539.1, Magic elevator. A715.2, Sun and moon born from a goddess impregnated by the wind; D1347, Magic object produces fecundity. D1610.2, Speaking tree. C710, Tabus connected with otherworld journeys. Motifs F51.1.1, Spider-web sky-rope, and F101.7, Escape from lower world by spider's thread, connect *Ibonia* to Indian tales. D2161.3.11, Barrenness magically cured. T584.0.1, Childbirth assisted by magic; C152.3, Eating tabus for pregnant woman; A511.1.2, Culture hero speaks before birth. A511.1.2.2, Culture hero in mother's womb indicates direction to be taken by her; T581, Place and conditions of childbirth. P10.1, Special place where occur births of royalty. T584.1, Birth through the mother's side; A511.1.1, Culture hero snatched from mother's side. Ibonia's birth, says Ottino, is also his circumcision (*L'étrangère* 555). F960.1, Extraordinary nature phenomena at birth of holy person. K2221, Treacherous rival lover. K1963, Sham magician. W117, Boastfulness. H41.5, Unknown prince shows his kingly qualities in dealing with his playmates; F611.3.2, Hero's precocious strength; F614.11, Strong man jumps across rivers. A163.1.1, Gods play chess. H1210, Quest assigned. H1500, Tests of endurance; H1543, Contest in remaining under water. A1101.1.2, Speaking trees. D1384.3, Charm gives safety on journey; D1541.0.1, Charms control storms. F628.1.4.1, Hero kills crocodile. H1165, Bullfight as task. H1501.2, Single combat to prove valour. D1840, Magic invulnerability. F911.6, All-swallowing monster. F913, Victims rescued from swallower's belly. E781, Life token. J1791.7, Man does not recognise his own reflection in the water. N825.2, Old man helper; K1941, Disguised flayer. D1317, Magic object warns of danger. H192, Recognition by supernatural manifestation. H32, Recognition by extraordinary prowess. H31, Recognition by unique ability. D610, Repeated transformation; D152.6, Transformation: man to kite; D142, Transformation: man to cat; D281.1, Transformation: man to wind. D866, Magic object destroyed. D1841.5, Invulnerability from weapons. L225, Reward refused by hero. B551.3, Crocodile carries man across river; B551.1, Fish carries man across water. The separation of the worlds is marked by Ibonia's passages over the river and his return dry-footed (D1551.6, Magic stick causes waters to divide). T100, Wedding. A1130, Origin of thunder. M341.1, Prophecy: death within certain time. Every motif, even a static one, functions to move the story along.

4.4 Structure

How do the parts of *Ibonia* — the words, images, minor genres — go together to make the whole? One answer would be that it belongs to a "tale type", a tale that persists in tradition.[12] It is more useful to see that this story is held together by a familiar kind of plot, which was first identified by the Russian formalist critic Vladimir Propp. His book *Morphology of the Folktale* demonstrates that one type of folktale, the fairy tale, found in one culture, Russian culture, has a constant compositional structure. Later scholars have found that this same structure is found in all Indo-European fairy tales, as well as in novels (both written and graphic) and films. Working originally from a random collection of 100 Russian fairy tales from Afanasiev's classic collection, Propp showed that each story could be divided into units he called functions. These functions are units of plot narrative action, larger than Thompson's motifs. Propp also demonstrated that there were only a limited number of these basic functions, thirty-one in all, and that they always occurred in the stories in a certain order. Not all functions had to occur in all stories, but if a story did contain, say, functions 1, 2, 6 and 7, then it would contain them in the order 1–2–6–7.

Distant though Madagascar is from Russia, *Ibonia* contains many of the plot elements that Propp found in Afanasiev's Russian tales. The numbered functions do not occur strictly in Propp's sequence, but even in his own limited corpus, as Anatoly Liberman points out (xxxi–xxxii), the sequence of functions is not always the same. To begin with, the birth of the hero is a preparatory section. The complication is begun by an act of villainy (Propp's term), namely Stone Man's abduction of the girl. Intermediary functions then lead to marriage. Propp's terms do apply to what happens in *Ibonia*.

Preparatory Section

Place: heaven. *Time:* unspecified.

Composition of the family: Sky Father, his son Heaven Watcher, his five married grandsons, and their wives.

Complication (the real beginning), 8a. *Lack:* Rasoa's barrenness; the need for a ruler to inherit the kingdom.[13]

---

12   The concept of tale type was developed by scholars who hoped to discover the origin and movement of every recurrent, recognizable plot. The authoritative catalog of tale types is by Hans-Jörg Uther; the best explanation is an encyclopedia article by Ulrich Marzolph.

13   Both the social order and the human domain suffer this lack of a ruler. In a myth, the lack would be cosmic: for instance there is no dry land until the waters which have covered the earth recede. In folktale and legend, the lack is social, a disequilibrium that must be rectified.

9. *Mediation:* by the diviner Ranakombe.

11. *Departure:* Rasoa goes in quest for a childbearing charm.

It was Propp who identified the "donor sequence" noted above. In function 12, the hero is tested or attacked, in function 13 he responds to the test, and in function 14 he either fails the test and is punished, or passes it and is rewarded with a magic object. Rasoa is the first to play the hero role.

12. *The first function of the donor:* she is assigned the difficult task of getting the charm.

13. *The heroine's reaction:* she succeeds.

14. *Provision or receipt of a magical agent:* she acquires the charm.

Certain functions, like Interdiction and Violation, occur in pairs. The master pair is Lack (the hero wants something) and Lack Liquidated (he gets it).

19. *Lack Liquidated:* she conceives and brings forth Iboniamasiboniamanoro.

Once the hero is born, there is a new beginning.

8a. *Lack:* Ibonia longs for his betrothed.

14. *Provision or receipt of a magical agent:* he gives power names to his weapons and ox.

9. *Mediation (the connective incident):* he consults the diviner.

11. *Departure:* he leaves home.

12. *The first function of the donor:* his endurance is tested, which prepares the way for his defeating enemies.

13. *The hero's reaction:* he passes the tests.

15. *Spatial transference:* Ibonia goes to Stone Man's village.

23. *Unrecognised arrival:* he disguises himself there.

27. *Recognition:* he begins to be recognised by Stone Man. He reveals himself to Girl of Grace.

16. *Struggle:* Ibonia and Stone Man join in direct combat.

18. *Victory:* Stone Man is defeated.

19. *Lack Liquidated:* Ibonia retrieves Girl of Grace, thus liquidating the initial lack.

20. *Return:* he returns home with his bride.

31. *Wedding:* Ibonia is married and ascends the throne.

The tale ends with a dual incident unknown in Propp's Russian tales, namely Ibonia's prescription of laws and his death, in accordance with his prediction. Most revealing of a cultural emphasis reflecting Merina values is the mother's quest plot, which makes a woman nearly as prominent as the hero.

4.5 The Combat Myth

One incident is essential to the structure. In a hero story, direct combat between hero and adversary is necessary (think of *High Noon, Bad Day at Black Rock,* or any other Western film). It is a story element that is truly worldwide, known as the combat myth. Traditional heroes around the world invariably face such combat. Anthropologist Clyde Kluckhohn found the combat myth in thirty-seven of fifty cultures which he studied for their myth themes. He interpreted the conflict psychologically:

> Not infrequently, the elaboration of the theme has a faintly Oedipal flavor. Thus in Bantu Africa (and beyond) a hero is born to a woman who survives after a monster has eaten her spouse (and everyone else). The son immediately turns into a man, slays a monster or monsters, restores his people — but not his father — and becomes chief. (163)

The Masikoro tale of Tsimamangafalahy (Text 12), like many African tales, turns the Oedipal theme into a son's avenging his father, thus making a place for himself to succeed him. In that tale, the combat myth is the decisive episode, whereas in Text 1, it is woven into a larger narrative structure. The reason a hero's story requires a combat is that his victory will set him apart from ordinary people and demonstrate that he is now a Man, eligible to marry.

Ibonia, in Text 1, resembles many a mythic hero in that he solves two problems. He prescribes laws; hence he is a "donative" hero, one who gives a necessary something to his people. He is also a "purgative" hero, because he rids his people of an awful threat (like the curse hanging over Thebes, in Sophocles's play of Oedipus). Ibonia rescues victims from the belly of an all-swallowing monster. Madagascar acquired this favorite motif (Thompson's F911.6) from Africa. With this episode, Ibonia can demonstrate his valor; with the successful combat, Tsimamangafalahy avenges his father's death by slaying the son of his father's murderer. Like most combat myths, the swallowing monster story is a fantasy in which a boy achieves identity as a man by means of a deed of manliness. One Greek myth, far more cosmic, portrayed "a chaos demon in serpent form, whom a god-champion overthrew in the earliest days of the world" (Fontenrose 230). This is true myth. The hero is the god of the world order (the cosmos); the chaos demon represents all moral and physical evil, which must be defeated for the world to endure. Chaos in African and Malagasy tales is less cosmic; the threat is to society. The demon is an ogre who swallows all the people and their livestock; by rescuing them the hero restores order and renews society.

In both "Tsimamangafalahy" and *Ibonia,* the hero's mother is a prominent character, brought on stage at the beginning with concern about her pregnancy. When the collector Cyprien Mandihitsy recorded the Masikoro tale of Tsimamangafalahy, in April 1986, the longings of the pregnant mother-to-be took up at least the first ten minutes of the performance. This emphasis is a particularly African touch, although stories around the world tell of a quest that is motivated by a pregnant woman's longings.[14] In a swallowing-monster story collected from a Sakalava informant on the west coast in 1907–1910 and published by Renel (1:117–119), a pregnant woman craves the liver of the mythical beast *kiridy* (a name meaning something like Tough), who has already swallowed people and animals. Her husband sets forth, traversing desert and crocodile-infested rivers, becoming hungry and discouraged. When he finally finds the *kiridy,* he shoots and misses; he is killed and swallowed. Back to the wife: she gives birth to a son (the hero), who grows precociously fast and strong. After his playmates say, and his mother admits, that his father was killed by the *kiridy,* he sets out with a gun in search of the monster, finds it, kills it, and begins cutting it open. From inside, his father says, "Be careful not to cut me with the axe, son" (echoing heroes like Ibonia who speak from inside their mother's womb). Opening the stomach, he releases all the people and animals. The Masikoro narrator performing this story spotlighted the pregnant woman by chanting this segment. Then when she went into the later episodes, where the father is challenged and defeated at the hands of his enemy, she switched to speaking (Mandihitsy et al. 19 n. 3). Her command of three registers — chanting, speech, and song — corroborates her skill in selecting and combining familiar narratives like the swallowing monster.

With an understanding of texture (the insertion of minor genres) and structure (the Proppian outline as a skeleton), we can move at last to Context.

---

14   Thompson's motifs H936, Tasks assigned because of longings of pregnant woman, and H1212.4, Quest assigned because of longing of pregnant woman.

5. Context, History, Interpretation

Translation gives *Ibonia* a new audience, which means a new context; it "re-contextualises" the epic. Context is basically of two kinds, social and cultural. A social context is needed for any performance. As Bauman says: "I understand performance as a mode of communication, a way of speaking, the essence of which resides in the assumption of responsibility to an audience for a display of communicative skill ..." (Story 3). Context of social situation is "the narrowest, most direct context for speaking folklore" (Ben-Amos 216). It entails a kind of microscopic study of oral performance that is available only to scholars who witness and record live performances. Written texts of course have a social context too, as seen in the headnotes in anthologies of literature: "Shelley composed this work in Italy between the autumn of 1818 and the close of 1819 and published it the following summer" (Abrams et al. 678). The production of the texts of *Ibonia* — its literary history — has been sketched above. Both literature and folklore are produced in a social context.

Context of culture is much broader, taking in all the topics of literary criticism: "the reference to, and the representation of, the shared knowledge of speakers, their conventions of conduct, belief systems, language metaphors and speech genres, their historical awareness and ethical and judicial principles" (Ben-Amos 215–216). Context of culture, for a translation into English from Malagasy, encompasses even more: the conventions of the "original" audience, the expectations of western readers, and all interpretations and critical commentaries. The historical context for interpreting *Ibonia* now is the encounter between Malagasy and European cultures. But that was also the context in which it was produced, back then. Once the British ships came over the ocean from Mauritius, cultural purity

DOI: 10.11647/OBP.0034.05

could no longer be assumed. It would have to be created, and the new literacy was the tool. So many times, in human history, imported tools have been employed by invaded peoples, who found ways to wield their traditional arts against cultural invasion, or globalisation. People who are economically backward and politically irrelevant are continually invoking native cultural traditions and mixing them with what is imported. Thereby they either resist the foreign or, more likely, create something new that is their own. Cultural creolisation is their weapon.

5.1 Context of Situation: Cultures Meet

In 1818 David Jones was a young Welsh missionary, sent with his family from the United Kingdom to Madagascar by the London Missionary Society (LMS). The LMS had been founded a generation earlier by Congregationalists (non-members of the established Church of England) to spread the Christian gospel to "the heathen", as Africans and Indians were known in those days. Especially eager to bring an end to the slave trade, LMS missionaries became active agents in creating friendly economic relations between Britain and Madagascar. The missionaries were not colonists; they wanted to proclaim the gospel and convert the Malagasy to Christianity, whereas the British government wanted economic and strategic advantages. The economic incentive was real enough. Through the Treaty of 1814, which ended the Napoleonic Wars, Britain had acquired Mauritius (the small island seven hundred miles away) from France. Mauritius was almost entirely planted in sugar. If its French and British colonists were to be fed, the island would need staples: rice, chickens, and cattle for meat. These necessities could come from Madagascar. So Robert Farquhar, governor of Mauritius, faced "a tricky situation", as historian Mervyn Brown puts it (133). He had to facilitate that kind of trade. At the same time another kind, the trade in slaves, increasingly unacceptable at home, had somehow to be stopped.

The Malagasy whom Farquhar and his envoy James Hastie had to deal with were the prominent Merina ethnic group, who lived in the capital city, Antananarivo. Merina still occupy the island's central plateau. It was only a couple of years before David Jones arrived that the Merina king, Radama I, began to welcome Europeans. Having inherited the throne at the command of his great father, Andrianampoinimerina, Radama too faced a tricky situation. Slaves were his main export. But in a treaty (1817) guaranteeing him British money and military hardware and naming him "king of Madagascar", Radama agreed to end the export of slaves. With arms and this new title, he could make true what he had told the British, that the Merina ruled the whole thousand-mile-long island.

At first David Jones liked the Malagasy enough to start schools for them: "I consider that the people in this country is [sic] in further civilisation than numbers in Wales ..." (qtd Gow 6). The ones he knew were not average; he dealt only with the Merina nobles (*andriana*) and freemen (*hova*) in the capital. Radama helped; he favored literacy. Once he and Jones discovered that to write Malagasy, Jones could use the Roman alphabet (the alphabet used in all European languages, the only alphabet he knew), Radama gave David Jones permission to open a school. Very soon, Malagasy boys were writing their lessons for him (the girls may have been in sewing class). Within a few years David Jones translated the Bible into Malagasy (from English, of course, God's language); he and his colleagues founded other schools; missionary artisans arrived to teach carpentry and other skills. Britain and Madagascar seemed ever so friendly. Literacy had arrived. I speculate that one of those young men, having gone through school, wrote down the tale of Ibonia.[15] Imagine him: newly literate, a product of a school operated by foreign men, many of whom were intolerant, even contemptuous, of the customs and traditions of his people (Gow 12–13). With his new skill he could resist the coming imperialism. He could honour the culture he came from by writing what had never been written — the life of a Merina hero, as he had heard it performed. Or was he himself an oral performer? The story glorified the Merina *andriana* [nobles]. Those who heard it performed, and those who would read it, must think of the royals and nobles they knew, Radama or Andrianampoinimerina. If these British were going to demand "complete adherence to a European standard of religion, dress, and general behaviour" (Gow 13), a large-scale product of Malagasy verbal art would keep the monarchic heritage active and alive.

His manuscript lay in family hands, as is the way with many Malagasy documents (who read it?), until another European missionary came along to uncover it as its editor. This was the Norwegian Lutheran Lars Dahle (1843–1925), who was inspired to collect folklore in Madagascar by the nationalistic example of other Norwegian folklorists of his time. For his

---

15   It has been speculated that the transcriber was an *ombiasy* [diviner], from the Antaimoro of the southeast, but there is no more hard evidence for him than I can give for a tradition-minded graduate of the LMS school.

countrymen Dahle wrote *Madagaskar og dets Beboere* [Madagascar and its People], in two volumes (1876, 1877). The person who owned the *Ibonia* manuscript gave it to Dahle, supplementing it orally in conversation (Dahle ix). That person was another voice in its multiple authorship. Dahle placed the long tale at the head of a section called *Angano na arira* [Tales and Legends], in his collection. He used Malagasy names for the various genres, but for the title of his book he used the new word Folk-lore, coined thirty years before by the Englishman William Thoms. Since its publication in 1877, Dahle's collection has been the point of reference for Malagasy readers and scholars seeking an understanding of pre-colonial Malagasy expressive culture.[16]

The context in which *Ibonia* was produced was the literary system of Madagascar. Every society has several modes of literary production, written and oral. Before David Jones made Malagasy a written language, the performance and reception of folklore was constituted by "structures of production, distribution, exchange and consumption" (Eagleton 47); these are what both folklorists and literary historians study. Folklore was produced and appreciated, if not systematically studied, all over the Great Red Island.

5.2 Context of Culture: Folklore in Madagascar

Madagascar is rich in folklore. There are myths of the origin of human beings and of death. There are legends about giants who left rocks and footprints that can be seen today. There are folktales of deformed and unpromising heroes, who accomplish quests and succeed where others fail. There are animal tricksters. There is an especially charming, inseparable pair of human tricksters, who collaborate on taking advantage of everyone else. There are innumerable proverbs; the collection by Father Paul Veyrières has over 6,000. There are riddles; there are the *hainteny* which Leonard Fox has translated. There are verbal charms. There is divination (consulting the supernatural). Dance, drama, art, and music are traditionally preserved

---

16   Classic though it is, Dahle's book should not have prevented further folklore research in Madagascar. Despite the collections by Charles Renel and Gabriel Ferrand, and the excellent monographs on Sakalava folklore by Émile Birkeli and André Dandouau, there was no effort until after independence to establish a systematic study of folklore. The failure is a stain on Madagascar's cultural history.

blinded it with their wings; when his uncle was about to try doing away with him, the crows woke the sleeping prince and he fled. The attempt to do away with him (which connects him with mythical heroes like Oedipus) is told as part of the royal histories of the *Tantara* (2, 74–75). Later, another bird showed him which direction to use in entering a town where he would find a wife. Then there was oratory: the rise of the great Merina art of oratory began to flourish after Andrianampoinimerina decreed that direct rule had to mean direct communication. Dispensing with intermediaries, he regularly took his case to the people, in huge assemblies which gave their name, *kabary*, to the oratorical genre. The shadow of this great king falls over Ibonia's whole life story.

5.3 The Hero Pattern

The ultimate origin of *Ibonia* lies outside Madagascar. It is a type of hero story which was already in existence by 9000 BC (Edmonson 150–154). Being so old, it diffused widely and shaped various kinds of narrative. Raglan gives one classic formulation of it (174–175), which I adapt: Ibonia's mother has no children, his father is a king, and the circumstances of his conception are bizarre. We are told almost nothing of his childhood, but on reaching his precocious manhood he goes in quest of his betrothed, to a kingdom that will become his. After his victory over the adversary (there is the worldwide combat myth), he marries her, becomes king, reigns uneventfully, prescribes laws, and dies. Does this sound familiar? The anthropologist Franz Boas observed, "Nothing seems to travel as readily as fanciful tales" (169).

The hero pattern represents the synthesis, or the ancestor, of myth, legend, and folktale. Generally folklorists define these genres separately. In Bascom's classic formulation, myths are "prose narratives which, in the society in which they are told, are considered to be truthful accounts of what happened in the remote past". Legends are stories "regarded as true by the narrator and his audience, but they are set in a period considered less remote, when the world was much as it is today". Folktales are not set in real time. They are "prose narratives which are regarded as fiction" ("Forms of Folklore" 8–9). By these definitions *Ibonia* is basically legend. Raglan believed (and never stopped arguing) that this pattern derives from a universal ritual; Joseph Campbell believed it was innate to humanity. Folkloric research discredits both these beliefs, and asserts that what explains the widespread distribution of hero stories is simply history.

"In the perspective of literary history [says Munro Edmonson], heroes are made, not born", and every language group sets in place the character of their hero (150). Scholars — Georges Dumézil, M. L. West, and Jaan Puhvel among others — have proved that the hero stories of ancient India, Iran, Greece, and Rome, as well as those of Teutonic, Celtic, and Slavic mythology, are all historically related, through the contact between peoples of different ethnic and linguistic traditions. The hero's traditional story was being narrated in these regions, in many different, varying forms and languages, long before people arrived in Madagascar. From the most ancient times, as people migrated across the Indian Ocean to Madagascar by way of Africa, maintaining their traditions of storytelling, they brought the hero with them. Just as they adapted rice cultivation to a new landscape, so they adapted ancient mythology to reflect new cultural emphases.

Other folk heroes in Madagascar are part of *Ibonia's* cultural context. Heroes cognate to Ibonia, who are abnormal "in excess or transgression" (Ottino "Mythology of the Highlands" 964), or who are strong, weak, or deformed, all coexist with him in the Malagasy repertoire. Our hero is one extreme of a range that includes tricksters, clever lads skillful in riddling, and a challenger rather like the Greek Prometheus. As he stands apart from all others except his betrothed, he calls to mind a Sakalava opposite, a culture hero who challenges God so successfully that he achieves equal rank with him, and donates the food supply to human beings. His tale is a myth (Dandouau 123–132), which *Ibonia* is not. Other culture-hero tales resemble *Ibonia* still less, for instance when they make the culture hero a trickster (as in some Native American folklore). Some tales connect the challenger, an earth-god, with the origin of death. He claims the bodies of the dead; the God who animated them claims the spirit. Thus the challenger completes the work of ordering human life and death. Still other Malagasy myths, not connected to *Ibonia*, reinforce this theme of shared responsibility for creation (Faublée 344–348, Michel 177). Of course Ibonia does reverse power relations, as these challengers do, but his epic adventure exists in the same repertoire with folktales in which a clever child talks back impertinently to a noble or answers a king's inquiry in riddles. In fiction, or on the shelves of the university library, these heroes are all contemporaries, but they were not all born at the same time. Genres of folk literature are born from other genres. The more secular, fanciful hero stories in Madagascar, and the later trickster stories, may well have been based on the more sacred and awe-inspiring narratives, imitating their features. Perhaps with the diminution of religious influence after Radama I's opening to the west, secularisation brought about more humorous and rational storytelling. Doesn't that always happen? Propp and other scholars have believed so. But no one knows.

5.4 Epic in Madagascar?

As we read it now, *Ibonia* is, in Isidore Okpewho's words, "fundamentally a tale about the fantastic deeds of a man or men endowed with something more than human might and operating in something larger than the normal human context and it is of significance in portraying some stage of the cultural or political development of a people" (34). By that definition, *Ibonia* is an epic. Like African epics and folktales, the story paints a wishful picture of its society and reinforces the social hierarchy. But can Madagascar, or Africa, actually produce an epic? At the time when the LMS missionaries were zealously collecting Merina proverbs, customs, and beliefs, they classified *Ibonia* quite reasonably as a fairy tale. It is fictional. It includes encounters with the supernatural and a clairvoyant diviner, as well as magic charms and objects. The hero successfully brings home the girl; he acquires extraordinary companions and a magic object that gives him victory. These were all folktale characteristics, well established by British folklorists like E. B. Tylor and Andrew Lang, who were contemporary with the missionaries (Dorson *British Folklorists* 187–265). Classifying *Ibonia* as a fairy tale was one mode of interpreting it. The editor Becker classified it with another term, from French literary history. "It is a sort of *chanson de geste*", he wrote, "repeated across the generations by Malagasy minstrels up to the fairly recent point when it was fixed in writing" (117 n. 3). A century later, Ruth Finnegan and John William Johnson debated whether there was such a thing as epic in Africa.

At the same time, fieldworkers such as Biebuyck were discovering new examples of oral performance that could only be classified as epics. It became clear that epic does exist among African peoples. The performers of Text 1 were not consciously imitating African models, but they independently arrived at, for instance, the same sort of hero tale as the Kimbundu (Angola) tale of Sudika-Mambi, which had been published by Héli Chatelain long before those debates. Sudika-Mambi (Thunderbolt) speaks from his mother's womb, is born with his weapons in his hand, undergoes many adventures in quest for a wife, dies and is resuscitated, and quarrels with his brother. Both *Sudika-Mambi* and *Ibonia* are heroic tales, with enough panegyric to expand them into epic. With these discoveries it was no longer possible to limit the notion of epic to Homer, Virgil, Ariosto, and Milton. Okpewho discovered common features in African and Mediterranean epics; Christiane Seydou went farther, reversing the canon to make African epics the norm which reveals constants of the epic genre around the world. At the same time, epic performances were recorded in India (Beck, Blackburn), which contributed to a redefinition of the genre on nonwestern models.

Always there is a correlation between social structure and folklore, as there is between social structure and musical style (Lomax). For the rise of epic in particular, two conditions in society have been postulated as necessary by René Étiemble. One is an organised, privileged caste of warriors or men admired for valour. That caste existed in Imerina, once Andrianampoinimerina had organised his guard of honour, "fifty, later seventy, warriors, including the twelve chiefs who had placed him in power" (Brown 125). Étiemble's other condition is a class of literate, dominating priests. In Madagascar, these would at first be the *andriana* [nobles], making common cause with foreign missionaries like David Jones. Like the African ethnic groups who produce epics, the Merina had "elaborate traditions of migration, expansion, and cultural assimilation [and] well-established traditions of conquest and warfare" (Biebuyck, "African Heroic Epic" 337). Later the oral histories transcribed by Father Callet created a Merina past in writing, as Elias Lönnrot had created a people's epic for Finland (Wilson 55–57). Callet's informants, says Ottino, were "theoreticians, careful to transpose into the operative terms of applied politics the theological and religious concepts of *Ibonia* and the cycle of the Andriambahoaka" ("Ancient Malagasy Dynastic Succession" 247–248). Other European members of this loose Malagasy quasi-priesthood were the Protestant missionaries like Richardson the lexicographer and Ellis the historian, not to mention the folklorists Sibree, Cousins, and Dahle himself. The social conditions sufficed to foster the composition of epic. With the emergence of a guard of royal protectors and a quasi-priestly class for royal tradition, the genre suddenly emerged in Imerina. Those who have heard or read dozens of shorter, less elaborated folktales may know, from this one example, that a long Malagasy epic narrative has existed. One could exist again, I suppose, but only if social conditions reverted radically into the past, which is not likely (Cole).

As this class of literate folklorists sedulously recorded dictation, were they and their informants acting against the interests of the

Malagasy people? The literacy David Jones and his fellows instituted, which was required to read the books by Callet, Dahle, and the rest of that quasi-priestly class, was not necessarily an instrument of subordination, but few indeed were the Malagasy who could read the books. As Edward Said has argued elsewhere, even their kind of cultural activity played an indispensable role in subordinating their people to Europe. By this argument, the *andriana* and *hova*, who opened Madagascar to European domination, become agents of oppression (72). Yet in their time they were the most progressive members of Malagasy society.

Commenting on *Ibonia*, Africanist scholar Harold Scheub points to its two directions of panegyric: "Its metaphorical power derives from measuring the subject against the ideals of the society, and it contrasts the hero with the 'flawed contemporary leader'". In its performance, Ibonia's tale "elicits pleasure through the recounting of his adventures" while pointing the hearer towards the grandeur of the past. "The hero is a quasi-historical figure, but the poem is historical and unhistorical at the same time" (12). Ottino specifies this ambivalence: "After episodes about the extraordinary circumstances whereby the first Malagasy royal dynasties were founded, [*Ibonia*] offers us a veritable philosophy of ancient sovereignty. The theoreticians of the *Tantara* translated these philosophical conceptions into technical rules for the choice and designation of sovereigns" (*L'étrangère* 415; "Ancient Malagasy Dynastic Succession"). Legend and oral history imparted the same philosophy.

5.5 Interpreters as Cultural Historians

If in this book, the translation is the text (shall I call it Text 16?), then all commentary and interpretation of the epic must be a kind of context. Interpretations of *Ibonia*, like interpretations of all literature, arise, in Madagascar and Europe, and are then succeeded by other interpretations. Often the last one claims to be superseding all the earlier ones, but in fact they do not cancel each other out. The array of interpretations is part of the context of culture for any work of literature, art, or music. The most valuable interpretations are pieces of cultural history, both of the people being examined and the writers doing the examining. "All epics", writes the great Africanist authority, "obviously provide rich, unsolicited information on the cultures and societies in which they occur" (Biebuyck "African Heroic Epic" 355). In that sense, folklore preserves the past into the present.

But preserving the past does not relegate the epic, or any folklore, to quaintness or obsolescence. Conceiving folklore as an accumulation of survivals from the past is itself a dying notion. Once, folklore was defined as consisting of survivals of past stages of the evolution of civilisation, from lower to higher. French colonists in Madagascar arrived with this assumption, which was part of the accepted master narrative of colonialism. With the rise of civilisation, they thought, folklore would disappear. After sixty-four years of French occupation (1896–1960), that did not happen, but back then, the collecting of folklore became urgent, because these survivals were a window into history. An exponent of this view was Georges-Sully Chapus (1887–1963), a great authority on Merina history and culture, who was well schooled in 1920s French anthropology. For Chapus, *Ibonia* was a narrative about history, which had been gilded. It was basically a story of the rivalry between two princes and their localities. Verbal artistry and variant forms of the tale held no interest for him; what was interesting was the array of surviving, archaic facts about the times before European contact. Realistic reflections of old Merina society in the text included the pastimes of the boys, the board game *fanorona*, the westward orientation of house doors, the groups working in the fields, and of course the deploring of a woman's barrenness. These were survivals from old times in Imerina. The hero's fantastic birth, and the elaboration of his naming, showed to Chapus the vital importance eighteenth-century Merina attached to the birth of a royal baby. So he read the texture closely, as he thought old Merina audiences would have done. What might seem to modern readers to be nothing but useless and fussy chatter, he said, was appreciated by the hearers as subtle, clever manipulation of language. Similarly, they valued the verbose discussion of Ibonia's encounter with Stone Man, because it demonstrates the versatile style of debate favored in old Imerina. The earthquakes, droughts, and tidal waves reflect the supernatural power of royalty. Chapus knew just what to look for in the tale. His interpretive mode required every folk narrative, no matter how fanciful, to have a historical kernel. When Chapus confronts an obviously fantastic detail like the life-token — the banana-tree planted by the hero as a signal to his mother that he is all right or has been defeated — he manages to convince himself that even this bit of fantasy, which turns up in Irish, Indian, and North American Indian folktales (Thompson's motif E761) is realistic, being a survival of an old belief. The old-time Merina must have believed in such things, according to what his contemporary, the eminent anthropologist

Lucien Lévy-Bruhl, called the "law of participation". The amulets which Ibonia carries to impart their magic force to his body, the force of Stone Man's talismans, the importance of divination, and the powerful role of the diviner Ranakombe — all these he interpreted as elements of primitive Malagasy religion.

Given his role as a French settler devoted to the interests of the colony, Chapus was bound to see the Malagasy as a primitive and superstitious people, whose history he would uncover. The *Ibonia* narrator's statements about destiny and fate, he says, come out of a host of superstitious beliefs in Merina narrative. Ranakombe's precautions, for instance, can do nothing against the oracular predictions voiced by the hero from the womb. Ibonia's pronouncements are predictions of what will happen, but they are also causes. So neither he nor his evil adversary Stone Man is morally responsible for his behavior. The decisive evidence that the old Merina were primitive folk, in Lévy-Bruhl's sense, was actually the mixed texture of the piece: natural and supernatural elements are mixed, because "Malagasy hearers were not shocked by the world of implausibilities contained in this tale. They did not distinguish the natural from the impossible" (Chapus 111) as modern Europeans do. Although Chapus speaks from that moment of Europe's history when colonised people had to be seen as mentally inferior, his researches do reveal information about Merina society.

Other interpreters use *Ibonia* as evidence for old Malagasy beliefs about the divine origin of royalty. For L. X. Michel-Andrianarahinjaka, traditional Malagasy thought denied any direct kinship between the creator and any race, real or imagined. That is why Ibonia dies like an ordinary mortal. Michel-Andrianarahinjaka believes that Malagasy folktales like *Ibonia* are of literary origin, and become anonymous only because oral transmission distorts them. The troubling consequence of thinking this way is to assume that there could have been no Malagasy oral tales before literacy, say before 1820. But it takes only one text, Flacourt's story of Rasoanor's overseas quest for a wife (Text 0), to disprove that. It is an old and discredited idea to say that folktales descended from an upper-class cultural elite to the common people, probably becoming cruder in the process. That could happen; cultural interchanges do occur, in all directions; but to assume that a downward flow is inevitable is nothing but ruling-class ideology. It presupposes a hierarchical class structure and denies creativity to ordinary people.

Cultural history finds every reason to look in *Ibonia* for kernels of older Malagasy thought. Divine kingship may be one kernel. The editor Becker — writing cultural history, despite adhering to the discredited idea of solar mythology — pointed to names like Railanitra, Heavenly Father, and Ifararangarandanitra, He Whose Gaze Remains Fixed on Heaven, as evidence for tracing the genealogy of this earthly prince back to heaven. Divine kingship remains an important strand of thought among the Sakalava (Feeley-Harnik). If, as Becker thought, the tale originated among them, the hero's genealogy was conceived to support the belief that kings are of divine origin. Like any Sakalava king, he changes his name at death. Like any ordinary Malagasy, Ibonia submits to mortality knowing that he will be reintegrated into the primary society, that of the ancestors. His story functioned to justify the claims to power of the *andriambahoaka* [princes].

What if *Ibonia* reveals remnants of ancient Malagasy mythology? This is the interpretive position of Ottino, who pioneered the vision of the Indian Ocean as a territory that connects, rather than separates, the islands around it. He sees the Southwest Indian Ocean islands — Madagascar, Mauritius, Réunion, Seychelles, and the Comoros — as "singular amalgams", constituted at different historical periods through the convergence of cultures. Ottino's ambitious programme is to extract the ancient strands of thought from this "preliterate 'Creole' civilisation" ("Mythology of the Highlands" 961). He writes: "Society, culture, religion, ritual, and institutions in central Madagascar, which largely determined kinship and political structures, may be regarded as the result of the rapprochement and combination of ZafiRaminia conceptions, which were Indonesian, and Antemoro conceptions, which were Sunni Muslim, moderately Africanised" (*L'étrangère* 520).[21] Malagasy culture results from a renegotiation of these heritages. Creolisation characterises early history on both sides of the Mozambique channel. To understand it, "Malagasy ideas and conceptions, whether comprised in myths and wondertales or in historical legends, must be systematically brought together with the Indian and Muslim religious, philosophical, and political representations that, from the thirteenth century on, converged across India on the Malay peninsula and the Insulindian archipelago, at the same time as Islam and the Bantu world were encountering each other on the shores of the east coast

---

21　The ZafiRaminia are thought to be traditional ancestors of some ethnic groups on Madagascar's east coast.

of Africa, producing what were to become Swahili civilisation and culture" (*L'étrangère* 576). So Ibonia bases his division of jurisdictions on influences from Indonesia, southern Africa, Islam, and India (*L'étrangère* 519–520). Ottino often seems to be saying, "Whatever you think Madagascar is, it's more complicated than that". Thus he foreshadows the more recent studies that advance creolisation as the central instrument of cultural creativity (Baron and Cara).

Fusing these diverse influences into a unified ideology takes Ottino into the politics of folklore. To reconstruct the connections of tales like *Ibonia* to Indian and Indonesian mythology, Ottino reads Dahle's anthology of folktales, *hainteny*, riddles, and folksongs as a more unified corpus than it is. In *Ibonia* and other wonder tales, which mythologise the origin of the upper class (*andriambahoaka*), the motive force is the necessity of ensuring that they shall have posterity. That is why Ibonia insists, all the way through, on retrieving only the wife of his destiny. Though at first that quest for a distant wife might seem to symbolise exogamy, Ottino says it is quite the opposite. Ibonia can marry only someone so close to him as to be nearly identical, symbolising endogamy.[22] "*I/ampela/soa/mananoro* is quite naturally destined for *Ibonia/masi/bonia/manoro*" ("Les Andriambahoaka" 84). Indian tradition is in the background when Ranakombe gives the baby boy the androgynous name Manly Princess: in the *Ramayana*, Ottino adds, the hero's quest for Sita can be read as a quest for his other half. Also, India possessed the image of a universal sovereign who is hermaphroditic; all through his story, Ibonia is only trying to recover his other half. In his semidivine person he unites earth, wind, fire, and water, the four elements which Madagascar inherited from Indonesia. If Ibonia is a divine king, who can control nature, ensure successful harvests, and make the waters divide before him, he can surely control human fertility. In this political interpretation, myths and tales are the discourse of the ruling class, the *andriana*. By mythologising the origin of princes (*andriambahoaka*), myths of their origin could mask that great shift in Merina society, the rupture between kinship structure as the source of power and the imposition of royalty, which was an institution the society had not yet known (Raison-Jourde 35). "Malagasy mythology", Ottino writes, "remains first and foremost a political mythology, through the use that has been made of it" ("Mythology of the Highlands" 974).

---

22   Exogamy is marrying outside your group, however that group is defined. Endogamy is marrying within it.

Ottino's historical approach sees the Great Red Island doubly. Madagascar is the result of a cultural renegotiation, which yielded a new and unpredictable civilisation; at the same time it is a tissue of ancient strands of thought, which have been preserved without change. At the end of the story, as the bard begins to move his audience out of the fictional world of his tale back to the waking life of the court, the parallels between Ibonia and historical Merina sovereigns become clear. The edicts of Andrianampoinimerina about marriage, which were well known to a royal audience, are a climactic episode of the *Tantaran'ny Andriana* (3:144–152; Delivré 31–33). The continuing immediacy of Merina concern about marriage across caste lines was underlined four years after Dahle published *Ibonia*, when Queen Ranavalona II promulgated laws regulating matrimonial alliances. Ottino traces this concern back to India (*L'étrangère* 556–578).

Interpreting *Ibonia* politically makes sense. It helps to explain why a young Merina would have felt an urgency to celebrate his people's hero. His tale would flatter the sovereign and members of the royal family, indirectly through inviting their identification with the hero's exploits and directly through praise poetry. It is the script of a state drama. As Shakespeare in *Macbeth* aimed at providing James I of England with an appropriate ancestor, Banquo, so the reciter of *Ibonia* sought to provide a Merina monarch with a forerunner. Repeated performances (if there were any) could be convoked by the desire of one or more of these *andriana* [nobles] to reassert claims of sovereignty, especially if the performer implied a family connection between the legendary hero and the living ruler. If the *andriambahoaka* [princes] were of divine origin, they deserved to rule over the *hova* and *andevo*. Thus the tale of Ibonia, like other Merina folklore, functioned in the classic way formulated by folklorist Bascom: "Folklore operates within a society to insure conformity to the accepted cultural norms, and continuity from generation to generation through its role in education and the extent to which it mirrors culture. To the extent to which folklore contrasts with the accepted norms and offers socially acceptable forms of release through amusement or humor and through creative imagination and fantasy, it tends to preserve the institutions from direct attack and change" ("Four Functions" 297). The subject of the epic was power; the intent was to remind Merina royalty of the glory of their past, and perhaps to incite them to some action in the present. No wonder that all through the era of British and French contestation over

Madagascar, the story remained popular as a remembrance of Merina heritage. That answers the question, "Why would anyone like this story?" It is their history, their entertainment, and their identity.

When we reconstruct the artistic communication and social life of a specific group, we go beyond the limitations of mere history-writing. The complex metaphor constituted by an epic tale attests to the creativity of people's responses to their circumstances. What anthropologist James Fernandez calls the "missions" of metaphor apply to this epic. One is to give people an identity, which *Ibonia* does by glorifying its epic hero. Another is to "move inchoate subjects into an optimum position in quality space", by which Fernandez may mean an audience's imagined living among the *andriambahoaka*. Another mission of metaphor is to enable an audience to take in images from the symbolic domain of the art-work. Fernandez gives an important place to transcendence, a "repeated search to 'return to the whole'", to capture all bodily and social experience, "out of dissatisfaction, perhaps, with the 'partness' of any of our devices of representation" (Fernandez 62). Consequently a capital mission of metaphor is to rescue people from an excessively narrow consciousness. The metaphoric "offer[s] both periodic and exceptional conversions" from being preoccupied with the part to an awareness of the whole. *Ibonia* carries out these missions. The epic holds up before its audience, and before us, a vision of the extraordinary potentials of human nature.

5.6 Why Translate It? Why Read It?

Why should a fantastic hero tale from a Malayo-Polynesian language be translated into English? Doesn't it restrict our attention to the problems and concerns of some faraway people we shall never know? Isn't it too local to be interesting? Admit that the story gave Merina hearers, a century or two ago, an imaginary relationship to something grander than themselves, a triumphal past, a glorious hero. Yet you might still decide that for us, *Ibonia* lacks transcendence — that it may appeal to Malagasy people, but it takes no one outside Madagascar into a realm of excitement or adventure or romance. Looking at the flow of languages and tradition-bearers around the world today, I do not agree. I see *Ibonia*'s vision of human potential as crossing the boundaries of language and ethnicity.

Translation of *Ibonia* into English waited over a century after Sibree wrote, "It is to be hoped that a complete version and translation of this exhuberant [sic] product of Malagasy fancy will some day be published with full illustrative notes, so that English readers may judge of the merits of this Ramayana of Madagascar …" ("Malagasy Folk-tales" 57). The primary text for my translation is François Noiret's revision of Becker, checked against Dahle's text of 1877. I especially want to reveal the narrator's oft-repeated *hono* [they say], which attributes the story to the ancestors. Like Ottino in *L'étrangère intime*, I break prose into verse when quoting from Dahle, but only in the presence of the two marks of elevated Malagasy style, antithesis and parallelism. As in so much of the world's oral literature, antithesis, balance, parallelism, and repetition of words and phrases are important devices of poetry in Madagascar. The extent to which the narrator relies on familiar *hainteny* patterns is an instance. The linguist-folklorist-critic-translator Dell Hymes sees such devices around the world. "Spoken narrative", Hymes writes, "has a level of patterning that is likely to be found everywhere, or nearly so …" (*Now I Know* 95). I attempt here to show the patterning of verbal art in a particular culture, so that the reader can summon up the voice of the performer and imagine the live performance of the piece. One can look, for example, for expressions like "and the rest", or "all the water creatures did the same", which probably are the written version of a direction to the performer to repeat verbatim a speech or list given earlier. Some lines, which looked to earlier editors like interpolations by a transcriber, are italicised. Finding such expressions is practice in folkloric restatement.

Every kind of study today — anthropology, comparative literature, psychology, information science — means taking possession of something "other" in language, social structure, politics, or art; it means translating that "other" into understandable knowledge about other people, and thereby about ourselves. The organisation of knowledge and the very concept of culture both require translation. Breaks in continuity and communication are everywhere. Mixtures of language, repertoires, and ways of speaking are everywhere. To think our way through the breaks and mixtures, we must explore what critic Homi Bhabha calls that "in-between space — that carries the burden of the meaning of culture" (38). Like any classic, *Ibonia* is timebound yet transcendent, projecting both a vision of the contradiction between past glories and present conflicts and an imaginative way to go beyond that contradiction.

Fig. 3 View from an estate on the east coast (Betsimisaraka Country).
Photo by Lee Haring (1976).

6. IBONAMASIBONIAMANORO
He of the Clear and Captivating Glance

There Is No Child

The Prince of the East, it is said,
was moved to pay a visit to his grandfather Sky Father.
With him he took his children:
    Gray Eyed Man
        Young Man Worth Six
            Manly Princess
                and his subjects, Many Cares and Many Close Ones.
Also   from The Kingdom of Many and The Valley of Many Trees
        he took along ten bulls and ten cows with their young.

The Prince of the North too was moved.
        He took with him To Be Powerful and Powerful's Father.

The Prince of the West too was moved.
        He took Smith of Silver Gods and To Be Powerful
        and his eight daughters.

The Prince of the South too was moved.
        He took Well Shaped Man and Cat With Big Mane
            and his eight daughters.
They wanted to visit Sky Father. They were his grandchildren.

DOI: 10.11647/OBP.0034.06

Their grandfather Sky Father, to welcome them
     picked   from his herds   oxen
          named Big One No Turning Aside and Big Wader.
Reunited with his grandsons, grandfather Sky Father said,
"I am pleased.
     No swine or curs will inherit my land."
Sky Father was happy
     he produced festivities
          he fired a cannon and a gun
               then he fed them.

Then came The Prince of the Center, the Great King-Maker,
     and his wife *Rasoa* [Beautiful-Rich].
Even the sky was stirred
          and the earth trembled where they passed
with their subjects The Clan of a Thousand Warriors
          and The Clan Gathering a Hundred Warriors.
Grass dried up
     herb stalks intertangled
          and the earth rumbled
               at the passing of the clan Too Many to Call.
The Prince of the Center too wanted to visit Sky Father
     being eldest of his grandchildren.

When the Prince of the Center arrived in his presence
     Sky Father said, "I am pleased, dear boy
          that you both came to call on me.
For the four who came before you
          I had the guns and cannons fire a hail of bullets.
The meal of welcome which I gave them was all fruitful things
          because they have many children.
But you I will treat differently.
I will order the guns and cannons fired
          I will have them loaded with one single stone
               and I will have them fired into the ground."
Then he sent for cattle   as the welcoming gift   and said,
"Take Glutton   take High Voiced Cuckoo

take Worth a Hundred Untied   take Worth a Hundred Not in the Forest,

take Restless   take Major   take Lazy Can't Lift

take Needs No Help Eating   take Handsome Silent

take Faraway Noise   take No Follower of the Just

take Shakes Like an Eel   take Oozes Bran Water

take Rattling Throat   take Voice Is Wealth

take Birds Nest in his Horns   take Manure on Head

and a hundred oxen and a hundred bulls.

Also take a hundred rams and a hundred ewes

a hundred fattened fowl and a hundred capons."

Then all these animals were gathered before him.

Sky Father now had begotten Heaven-Watcher,

who had begotten those five brothers —

Prince of the East

Prince of the West

Prince of the North

Prince of the South

and Prince of the Center.

Then Sky Father said, "Bring Heaven-Watcher,"

(he was not there before)

"and I will offer the meal of welcome for my children

Prince of the Center and Rasoa."

When Heaven-Watcher came, he called his five sons.

They approached him.

Sky Father then went out to mount his golden throne.   He made a speech:

"Now I have readied the gifts of welcome for the four men

but not for Prince of the Center.

We will set two groups facing each other.

That means a hundred bulls, a hundred oxen and the rest.

I have had the guns and cannons fired with a single charge

and the discharge was lost in the earth

because there is no child to cry.

Rasoa is barren!

Prince of the Center has fathered no child.

What I have to say to you then

Rasoa and Prince of the Center   is this:

All is well
   excellent is your greatness
                                 but there is no child to cry."

Her Quest for Conception

Now when Rasoa heard that   she was upset.
She wept
      she cried out
         she flooded her husband with tears down to his neck
            that Prince of the Center.   Then she said
"Prince, look at all the riches here
      look at all the wealth
         only a single calabash is denied us,
and swine and curs must inherit this kingdom and this land."

"I will take no second wife," said Prince of the Center.
"Go you
   Get help from *Ranakombe* [Great-Snake], the diviner
      get from him a childbearing charm."
So Rasoa set out to get help from Ranakombe.
With her she took ten women
      and a hundred men carrying guns, spears and muskets.
When they reached Ranakombe's place   Ranakombe said
"The 'line for two' is not made by my foot
      The 'line for four' is not made by my hand.
What will happen next year   I see this year
what will happen tomorrow   I see today.
So I know   even before you open your mouth
         what brings you here   grieving
            it is your need for a child.
How many men are with you?
      How many women are with you?"
Rasoa said, "A hundred men
      carrying a hundred guns, a hundred spears, and a hundred muskets
         and ten women carrying ten round stones."
"Aaayyy!" said Ranakombe.

"A formidable man will he be on earth.

In your womb a thousand men,

inside you one hundred men

ten years will you carry him, O Rasoa.

If you will agree   then that is what I give you.

If you will not agree   you will have no other child.

Go home, then

for he is a disaster child

disaster, that one

a calamity child.

He is thunder   he is lightning

on earth he will kill his father

in the womb he will kill his mother."

Then Rasoa said, "Ahhh —

it is bad to have nothing   even disaster."

Ranakombe said, "So be it. If you agree, then go you to Male Rock of Thousand Corners.

There will be lightning

there will be animals

there will be deadly things.

When you go there

have each of your women carry two cannonballs

and you carry three.

A locust you will get there   as your childbearing charm.

There a thousand strong men will meet you

but those thousand strong men will flee

for that one locust will be a raging bull

thus you will pass over the Male Rock of Thousand Corners."

Then she set out.

When she arrived near the rock

waterspouts   winds   thunderbolts   hail   fell upon her.

So did all deadly things.

Seven times did the ten women fall

but Rasoa was the only one who did not fall.

As she approached Male Rock of Thousand Corners,

there were more deadly things.

When she came to the north of the rock,
>> there was the locust, on top of it.
Male Rock of Thousand Corners sank down level with the ground.
Again did her ten servant women fall   crushing their hands
>> but only Rasoa did not fall.
The locust was bombarded with bullets
>> so that Rasoa could catch it
>>> but that locust did not die.
It seemed ever more alive, to look at him.
Then Rasoa bound up her loins like a man
>> to catch the locust
>>> and she did catch the locust.
It carried them up, flying.
>> Rasoa almost reached the sky
>>> but she would not fall
>>>> she was sitting atop the rock.
Then it came down to earth
>> but did not enlarge its hole
>>> it fell into the same place as before.
Rasoa slid into the stone
>> and took the locust to make a childbearing charm.

Then each of the oldest trees in the world began to speak:
"I am the childbearing charm."
>>>> "*I* am the childbearing charm."
When Rasoa had arrived among the childbearing charms
>> among Does Not Wither When Transplanted
>> and Does Not Dry When Planted
>>> Thousand Goat Horns
>>> Hundred in the Womb
she went into the forest to get Single Trunk.
> But when she reached the top of Single Trunk
> it was the locust who seized the charm.
Then did Rasoa return   traversing spiderweb to spiderweb
>> not touching the sky
>>> not touching the blossoms on the trees as she passed
>>>> not walking on the ground.

Then the childbearing charm
           that Rasoa procured in the forest
showed itself to the prince in the village   and said
"Say your prayers, for Rasoa is in battle.
     Your praying should be like this:
       'Win the day! Bring forth our man!
         This eel must not be confined.
         No ditch water will hold him.'
    Make your prayers so."   Then came Rasoa
and settled in her own village   called Iliolava [Long-Standing].
Its stones smashed each other
    its grass dried up.
That was a town that could withstand anything.
     Hence its name, Long-Standing.

The Locust Becomes a Baby

When Rasoa came to the village
    her thousand men went to gather firewood
      to roast the locust and give it to her to eat.
When the firewood had come
    they lit all of it at once   in one hearth
      and roasted the locust there.
The locust shone fiercely there in the flames.
    High did the fire blaze   yet it was not cooked.

Then she sent for Ranakombe.
But even before her messengers reached him
    Ranakombe had a vision.   He said
"Now then, Clever Slave Girl, what is that in the east?
    The 'line for two' is not made by my foot
    The 'line for four' is not made by my hand.
What will happen next year   I see this year,
    what will happen tomorrow   I see today."
The girl went to look and said, "See!
Seven men are coming from the east.

They hasten with their spears
they brandish muskets."
"Ah," said Ranakombe
"they are from Young-Woman-with-Disaster-Child."
When the messengers reached his place, he said
"I understand the unsignified
I know the unsaid.
How many men have blown the conch?
How many men have fired muskets?
How many men have beaten drums?
How many men have gone for firewood?
How many men have fought bulls around the house?
How many men have killed bulls?"
And they said,
"None of that has been done, grandfather."
Then said Ranakombe to them
"First, go bring together a thousand fighting bulls
a thousand muskets to shoot
a thousand conches to blow.
Seventy drummers
thrice seven bulls for slaughter
a hundred rams for slaughter.
As for me, I wait until the Friday of the new year
until the end of the month of Alahamady
a bad month for the king.
Then is the new king enthroned
decrees are executed in the capital
no one is unjustly killed.
For that child has a potent fate.
I will not take that day lightly
I will not offend the year
lest I be reproached.
Go you now back to Rasoa."

When the messengers returned to Rasoa
they told her his words
so that they could gather all those things
before Ranakombe arrived.

On that Friday, Ranakombe set out for Rasoa.
When he was at her door, he said
     "Fire the cannon around the village.
 On the east slope of the hill, put up The Only Uplifter
     and The One With Many Victims [idols]
       and the golden musket."
The cannon was fired around the village.
    A thousand bulls fought around the town.
There was shouting and rejoicing.
     Then were killed the hundred rams
       and the thrice seven bulls.
(The two idols were placed east of the village because the boy's rival lay that way.)
Only then did Ranakombe enter the house of Rasoa
     to approach the locust.
When he stepped over her threshold
     the locust broke away from the hearth
      and went to the ridgepole of the house.
 Fire spread before Ranakombe and the locust.
Then Ranakombe gave orders   saying
"I see that child is disaster
    I see that child is calamity
    I see a formidable man on the earth
yet I am the one who gave him to Rasoa of Iliolava.
 If you are not to come to term
      go south or north
      and do not throw yourself into the fire.
 But if you are to become human
    to be an unstoppable animal
      to be a unique ruler   then
      throw yourself into the fire."
And the locust dropped into the fire   and was cooked.
No one took him out.
 He jumped out of the fire
   and perched on the head of Rasoa
     then pierced her head   settled in her womb
      took shape   and became a child.

And when the baby was formed in Rasoa's womb
    then the ten bulls and the hundred rams were killed.
Rasoa ate them all herself.
    From then on she ate no more
        she allowed only wind in her mouth   until her baby's birth.
            Ten years was the baby in her womb.

The Baby Chooses a Wife and Refuses Names

When Ibonia had been three years in Rasoa's womb
    the baby demanded a wife   saying
"Iampelasoamananoro, the Girl of Grace, is my wife.
        See that she is not stolen by some dangerous man."

                                                    But Rasoa said,
    "You are still only a seed. How can you choose a wife?"   And the baby said,
"I know   I know, mama   I am a seed
        but I am plighting myself while still a baby
        I am marrying while still a seed.
    Also: I want no other woman
                    I give my name to no other woman
                        and I favor no other land or person.
    If Girl of Grace dies   I will not bury her in the ground
        and if she lives, I will not leave her to any man.
    Behold: a Nothing Man Looking for Trouble
        Owner of Big Estates
            Owner of Properties Spread Wide
                is making trouble.
    He wants to take my wife"   said the baby.
    So from his mother's womb the baby said
"Call the nobles of Iliolava!
        for Girl of Grace has been abducted
            by a dangerous man with powerful charms.
    She has been stolen by Stone Man Trouble.
    Cry out!
            Say, 'She is stolen by Stone Man Trouble!
                Stolen by Stone Man!
                    Stolen by formidable Stone Man!'

He may be trouble
   but I am disaster" said the baby.
So the people of Iliolava went in pursuit of Girl of Grace
   but they could not catch her.
And the baby said in his mother's womb
"They did not catch Girl of Grace, mama.
   The villagers are back."

Boasting Before Birth
When ten years had passed   the pregnant Rasoa
 happened to be among some planters.
The baby became heavy
   she began to feel pains. And the baby said,
"Take me home, mama.
   I am no *tako* leaf   floating on water
I am no sweet potato top   my own opposite
   I am no hog   puffing myself up
I am no *tenrec* [hedgehog] rolling myself up
   I am no dog   with dangerous tongue
I am no locust   parading myself
   I am no hedgehog whose prickles can't prevent death
I am no stone   that starts rolling
   I am no banana   one is enough of those
I am no fog   covering the earth
   I am no cock   waking in the morning
I am no guineafowl carrying off my own young
   I am no crocodile waiting at the ford.
I am an edible arum in the chink of a rock
   not crushed with the foot
     its leaves not eaten.
Pass over it   your knees swell up
   look at it sideways you lose an eye
    point at it   you lose fingers.
Place it on the flame a calamity
   cook it   a disaster.

But I am a poisonous creeper from beyond the sea
        pass under it   it blinds you
            step over it   your stomach swells up
                leave it there   it makes your toes drop off.
I am an enormous crocodile lying in wait at the ford.
            if a pirogue strikes him   he capsizes it
                anyone crossing   he chews his stomach.
I am a big house seen from afar.
    Not even a whole crowd can take it apart
            but if they do   it takes revenge.
    And when those from across the sea catch sight of me
            I add them to my servants.
I am one dangerous lad!
            I will destroy my rivals' lands
                while my lands are already mine"
                            said the baby in his mother's womb.
"I excel, mama"   he said.
"Fix a time for me   I am not there
            at a time fixed by me   I am there.
    When I need something   I get it
                something needed from me   they get nothing.
    When I strike someone, any season   he dies, any season
            when I give someone life, any season,   he lives, any season.
    Easy it is to believe that I am alive
            hard to believe I am dead.
    Here am I   me alone
            here are numberless united warriors
                a thousand defiant men
                a hundred united men.
    A thousand pirogues could not invade my realm, Mama
            a hundred pirogues could not capture me"   he said.
                                Then said his mother
"You all alone? A thousand pirogues   a hundred pirogues?
    Ah, this one is fatal   to his mother   in her womb
            fatal to his father   on the earth."
                                The baby went on,

"I do not insult those who love me
    I use no bad words to those who leave me alone
  but I return insult for insult
    I use bad words to those who use them on me.
For when sweet words come to me
      then those people are my friends
        even those who live beyond the sea,
          indeed those who live above the sky.
My feet were not made by man
      my hands were not made by man"   he said.
"Mine is the earth   heaven is Sky Lord's.
He is Sky Lord above   I am Sky Lord on earth.
 If sweetest words come to me   I speak the sweetest words
if foul words come to me   I speak foul words.
      Only I am the one who can fill the earth."

His Quest for a Birthplace

"Now   go all over the world"
            said the baby from his mother's womb.
And the baby led Rasoa to a bare rock
    to look for a place to give birth.
And from Rasoa's womb   the baby said
"I do not like it here, mama.
    It is where kites nest and eagles are born.
Kites eat chicks   are the pride of their owners
   curses follow them   but only make them stronger.
Eagles [*vorohamery*, strong birds] I know are strong.
    What they carry off —
      those that escape get their due
        those they catch are finished off
      from their claws nothing falls.
Take me away.   Let us go, mama.
I hate this place.   It is a place for plunderers
   strong only because they work with their claws.
They have no subjects to call up
   no subjects to dispatch.
      Here I can not rule."

So they left that rock.

    She kicked it   it shattered.

Again the baby led his mother away.

     She came to the summit of a high, high place.   The baby said

"I like it here, mama.

     This is where I will be born.

 This is the highest of places

     where many look up for help

       and there are many to muster."

Then he changed his mind, saying

"I like it here, mama

     but it is a place of ghosts and spirits

       and for that I do not like it.

 Good and bad winds blow here together."

Then his mother arose and left that place.

     She kicked that hilltop

       the earth shuddered

        the rocks rolled and were crushed.

They set forth again, and the baby made his mother traverse all the forests of the earth.

Though still in her womb

     he led his mother   and again he said

"Oh, mama, I do not like it here.

     A thousand people rule here.

     The small lead the great.

There is nothing solid here.

 It is a land of wild dogs

    a land of lemurs

     a land of wild hogs

      a land of wild beasts.

Take me back, mama. I hate it here.

It is a land of the stealthy."

And again she arose

     again she kicked the forest.

     The trees were uprooted   pulled up   overturned.

They set forth again   and came to water   to find a birthing place.

His mother submerged in the water. Then he said
"I do not like it here, mama.

    Here are many slippery creatures
        I do not know how to manage them.
    Here I can not rule."
So she arose, and left the water creatures there.
She stirred up the water   It dried up
    The creatures in there got stirred up by the waves
        and floated on the surface.
But his mother did not come out of the water just yet,

                      for he said,

"I like it here, mama.
  It is a bed with a soft mattress
    I need not look for mattress or pillow.
 And yet I do not like it, mama,
    it is a big mat that cannot be rolled up,
      a *lamba* [shawl] that cannot be folded,
      a pillow that cannot be carried."
So she arose again and blew on the water
        (and that, it is said, is what makes waves on the sea).
Then his mother went straight back to the village.
When she reached the village
    he guided her to the ridgebeam,   saying
"I like it here, mama,
  because of the thousand men suspended
    and the three men separated.
Here there are many to respect me   many to support me.
Yet I do not like it
    because leaning on so many
      prevents my ruling alone.
Most of these slaves are strong only in talk.
    Impossible to exercise justice.   So take me down, mama."
Now his mother went to the south gable   but he said,
"This I detest, mama.
  It is for sacrificing cattle to the dead
    and exorcising for the living.

Take me to the north gable."

When his mother reached the north gable, he said,

"Oh, mama, I detest this.

It is for calling on *Zanahary* [creator].

If there be any good place, it is here.

In the beyond all are brothers and sisters

but on earth there is deceit,

and no loyal combat.

So take me to the east wall, mama."

When his mother reached the east wall, he said

"Now this is a good place, mama.

Yet it is refused by those of the south

and those of the west.

It is one body lying down, supported by the many.

I see no order in this reclining sir

he is not very terrible."

Again his mother moved.   Again he said

"Carry me to the tie-beam, mama.   That is the auspicious place.

It has ten thousand umbrella-carriers

a thousand porters

a hundred men united."

And from inside his mother   he added

"See where the sun is."   His mother said

"The sun is right over the house."   And the baby said,

"Now is the moment for the cat to steal, mama

now he robs the sky,

now he robs the east,

now he robs the west,

now he robs the south.

Now to add all those to my ownings, mama,"   he said.

And from his mother's womb he said

"Have four thousand guns fired in the four directions.

Have them fire a thousand shots to the sky

First toward heaven."   They were fired toward heaven.

"Now, have the guns been fired, mama?"   said the baby.

"They have been fired," said his mother.   And he said

"Those men! It's as if they'd been fighting for ten days, mama.
  Now,   have the shots fired to the four points."
            They were fired.   And he asked
"Have they been well fired, mama?"
His mother said, "They have not been fired. Only the east one has been fired."
                                    Then the baby said
"Now is accomplished the oath of fidelity with the people, mama.
  The land is ours now   and no shot has been fired.
      This grip will last all the day.
  Now will I be born, mama
      there is the throne you will lie on," said the baby.
        "There is the golden throne I will mount
              seven meters wide   fourteen meters long."
When the baby was about to be born, he said,
"Take fire
      make it blaze up in the hearth
        make a sharp knife   and swallow it in a banana.
  For I will not come out above   or below
        I will come out through your stomach, mama."

Ibemampanjaka [Great King-Maker] said
"Is not this the thing I do not want, Rasoa?"   But Rasoa said,
"What is bad is to have nothing.   Even if he is trouble
      this baby is the heir to the land."
  So Great King-Maker made a sharp knife
      and put it in a banana
        and Rasoa swallowed it.
  Then the baby took the knife
      and while Rasoa was still on the throne
        he opened her womb and came out.
  Then the baby jumped up on the golden throne.
      His mother died there on that throne
        and he turned her head toward the east.
On the day of his birth   all living beings, whatever they were
      were broken up.

Rocks split open
the ground turned over
the sky rumbled.

That is how earthquakes first appeared.

Yet Unnamed

The servant Hated By the Hearth came to Great King-Maker and said
"Rasoa has given birth
but the mother has died on the throne."
Great King-Maker was shaken.   He said
"Call my man Not Shielded from My Call
and have him get a thousand women to bathe this baby."
When the thousand women arrived from Iliolava
they entered the house and came forward to pick up the baby.
One came up to hold him   he kicked her and broke her leg.
Another came   he kicked her and put out her eye.
Some had their teeth knocked out   some had their hands cut off.
And when his father came to pick him up and bathe him
he kicked him and broke his leg.   His father said
"Ah, this baby means disaster   means trouble.
In the womb he was fatal to his mother
on earth he is fatal to his father."
Then the baby came off the golden throne
and jumped into the blazing fire.
To help him, they threw water on the fire
but that did not stop it   instead it flared up.
Then they tried to pick the baby up
but he was slippery   could not be held
and hot as the fire was,   it did not bother him.
Then said Great King-Maker to Rasoa's sister Endriavelo [Shadow Mother of the Dead],
"This will not do. Go to Ranakombe
take a thousand men with muskets and spears
and ten women to go with you." And she went.
Just at that moment Ranakombe said
"Is that you   crying out of the fire   and bothering me?

I understand the unsignified   I know the unsaid."

Then Endriavelo came to Ranakombe. Ranakombe said, "I know your errand.

     The 'line for two' is not made by my foot,

     The 'line for four' is not made by my hand.

Rasoa has given birth

     a thousand people have been killed

        a hundred people wounded.

Aahh   this will not do.

Send a thousand men for firewood

     and give the baby the first wood they find.

Then the fire will blaze up   for that baby must have a name."

His man left and did what Ranakombe said.

Refusing Names from Princes

Then Ranakombe set forth   and reached Iliolava.

When he reached the door   the baby cried once, "Ahhh!"

     then he was silent and did not speak.   Ranakombe said,

"Go get four bulls from the Herd of a Thousand

     and kill them at the four points of the earth

     and get four thousand men from Iolava

       to fire the cannon while this baby is bathed."

The four bulls were killed

     the four thousand mouths of cannon

       were fired towards the four points of the earth.

Only then did Ranakombe speak a name for the baby. He said

"Shout, men! shout, men!

Here is the name I give this boy: Male Big-Winged Kite.

Offered or not   he steals in the owner's sight

     he plunders in his father's sight

      he steals in his mother's womb

Curses aimed at him only make him stronger.

Look at him sideways   like the ground where you slip and fall

He goes no distance to cut up his meat

     he does it on his victim's head.

That is one formidable man"   said Ranakombe.

But the baby ran all round the house.

He did not want that name.

"Slow, that baby is," said Ranakombe.
"I will give him the name Lord-Eagle.
A great plunderer
　　　but he does it only in a thousand men's sight
　　　　　not in sight of the few.
Those who escape him get their due
　　　in the end they are put to rout.
What is in his claws does not fall.
　　　　One like that is enough to swallow the earth."
"I like that well enough, father," said the baby.
　"But that creature is a chicken thief
　　　so after all I won't have it."

"Slow, that baby is," said Ranakombe.
"Shout, men! shout, men!" said Ranakombe,
"I will give him the name Lord Friday's Hog.
Unprovoked　　　he thunders
　　　without rubbing　　　he lights a fire
　　　　with no axe　　　he cuts
　　　　　with no spade　　　he digs.
He descends into valleys without making a path
　　　he crosses the hills without shoes
　　　　as if he had eight hundred piles of manioc.
He clears his path in the bush
　　　where there are eight thousand stalks of fern.
Those he has not caught　　　are unheard-of
　　　those he catches are lifeless,　　　useless."
"Ehh, I do not want that one, father," said the baby.

"Slow, that baby is," said Ranakombe.
"Shout, men! shout, men!" said Ranakombe
"for I will give this baby of mine the name Prince Drenched Cuckoo.
He flies, but not high
　　　he travels, but not far

he eats slowly

he does not touch rum.

He has a hundred small silver needles   a thousand big ones

he wakes up at the conch

he swallows a bull in one gulp.

That is a formidable man on the earth."

"I do not want that one, father," said the baby.

"It is the sign of an abortion."

"Slow, that baby is," said Ranakombe.

"Shout, men! shout, men!" said Ranakombe,

"the name I will give this baby is Prince Who Sits Like a Frog.

He is a thousand men of doom,

ten thousand men of one mind

a hundred men united.

All he does is croak   yet his howls split the earth."

"Eh, I do not want that one," said the baby.

"He likes to stretch out.

Fearful people pass over his head,

cowards insult his wife.

I do not want that one, father," said the baby.

"Slow, that baby is," said Ranakombe.

"Shout, men! shout, men!" said Ranakombe,

"the name I will give this baby is Prince Owl Terror by Night Quiet by Day.

He makes night into day and day into night.

All by himself he swallows an ox.

He needs no knife to cut it

he needs no chopping knife to slice it

he

just

swallows."

"I do not want that one, father," said the baby.

"Slow, that baby is," said Ranakombe.

"Shout, men! shout, men!" said Ranakombe.
    "I will give this baby the name Big-Maned Cat.
  He raises his head like a man
      he has the loins of a formidable man
        he has the feet of Big-Hunter
          he kills with only his voice.
  He takes what is under his axe
      as if it were under his leg.
  He eats no meat   but he drinks blood.
  That is a formidable man on the earth.
  The one he kills one day   dies that day
    the one he kills at night   dies that night."
"I do not want that one, father," said the baby.

"Slow, that baby is," said Ranakombe.
"Shout, men! shout, men!" said Ranakombe,
"I will give this baby the name Prince Giant.
  He bathes and does not smell bad
      swims and is clean.
  Unchallenged in his village
      he is master of many servants
        breeder of many fattening oxen
          a sugarcane with young shoots.
A hundred dogs can not swallow his fingernail clippings
      ten thousand can not swallow his toenail clippings.
The tenrec lodges in the hair of his armpit
      hedgehogs nest in his eyebrows
        little birds lay their eggs in the hair of his nose
          crows lay their eggs in the hair of his head
            guineafowls give birth in the hair on his neck.
His leg can wash clothes
  his leg can sharpen knives
His knees are anvils
  his fists are hammers
    his fingers are tongs
      his calves are bellows.
He brags, 'Put it on the fire   put it on the flame
  take it off   take it off.'

He eats a hundred rams
　　he eats ten bulls at a time.
What cannot be eaten he cuts up
　　what cannot be cooked he puts on the fire.
He cuts without a knife
　　he slices without an axe.
That is a formidable man on the earth," said Ranakombe.
"I do not want that one, father," said the baby.

"Slow, that baby is," said Ranakombe.
"Shout, men! shout, men!" said Ranakombe,
"I will give this baby the name Smith of the Silver Gods.
He is a formicable man on the earth
　　he makes a thousand bulls fight
　　　　he eats a hundred bulls at a sitting.
He is a descendant of Rich Man
　　a son of Owns No Little.
He steals from another
　　he gathers up what is not his own.
What he takes cannot be taken back
　　because he is disaster man."
"I do not want that one, father," said the baby.

"Slow, that baby is," said Ranakombe.
"Shout, men! shout, men!" said Ranakombe,
"I will give this baby the name Handsome Gray-Eyed Man.
Now　　　he is a formidable man on the earth
　　he takes what is not his
　　　　he steals right from the owner's hands.
He is a descendant of chiefs
　　a child of Kills This Very Day.
The places he goes　　　all is not well there
　　but smashed to fragments."
"I do not want that one, father," said the baby.

The Name for a Perfected Man

"Slow, that baby is," said Ranakombe.
"Shout, men! shout, men!" said Ranakombe,

"I will give this baby the name Manly Princess.
  With a woman's name   he is formidable on the earth.
  She is a descendant of Killer
      daughter of Life Giver
          descendant of Sharer
              daughter of Giver
  a descendant of Gold Being
      daughter of Silver Being.
  Hard to believe she were dead
      easy to believe she is alive.
  Loved by the thousand
      honored by the hundred
          a hundred men united
              a thousand men of one mind.
  Those she kills one year   die the same year
      those she gives life to one year   live that same year.
  Descendant of Rich Man   daughter of Great Herds.
  When she looks up   the sky opens
  when she looks down   the earth opens.
  She kicks a rock   it shatters in ten pieces.
      She bathes   that is a rainy day
          she does not bathe   that is drought."
"Ah, father, I could almost like that one," said the baby
      "but something in it I do not like."

"Slow, that baby is," said Ranakombe.
"Shout, men! shout, men!" said Ranakombe
"I will give this baby the name Father of Powerful One.
  Now he is a formidable man on the earth
              descendant of Rich Man
                  son of Much Coral
                      grandson of Great Riches.
  He makes a thousand bulls fight
      eats ten rams at a sitting.
  Son of Ever Generous   grandson of Always Giving Away
      child of Always Handing Out   from the lineage of Never
      Gives Little."
"I do not want that one, father," said the baby.

"Well!" said Ranakombe. "What name do I give this baby?

Shout, men! shout, men!"   said Ranakombe,

"for the name I will give this baby

 is The One of the Clear Captivating Glance [*Iboniamasiboniamanoro*].

What is there   he leads

        what is here   he leads.

What he demands   he gets

        what is demanded from him   no one gets.

At any time appointed   he is not to be found

        at a time he appoints   he is there.

He can manage matters of wealth.

He looks up   the sky opens

        he looks down   earth opens.

He points to the east   it overturns

        he points to the north   all offspring are destroyed

                he points to the west   all go barren

        he points to the south   swarms of lice attack   like chickens.

No way to fight him

        no way to escape him.

 He does not need two nights' sleep

        he needs just one to go into battle.

The sky trembles   the earth shakes

        waters dry up   hills crumble

                in the path of this formidable man.

He is descended from Great in Length

        son of Great in Width

        descended from Golden Being

                son of Silver Being

                        child of Giver

                                grandchild of Scatterer.

Descended from Ordered Being

                child of Cutter

                        grandson of Big Cattleman

                                a child of Many Fattened.

Descended from No Need to Breed To Have Cattle to Kill

                son of No Dependent

                        grandson of Creditor.

Those he kills one year   die that year
     those he gives life to one year   live that same year.
His royal power has no equal
     his authority no one shares
          it befits only him.
He scorns what comes from others
     even from beyond the roaring sea
          but he is scorned by none.
Grandson of Unique Prince   son of Only Possessor
     no one can be found to fight him.
 He it is who pacifies the earth   that formidable man.
Beasts are beasts
     crocodiles are crocodiles
          but he is a huge crocodile lying in wait at the ford.
A pirogue strikes him   he overturns it
     whoever crosses   he bites his stomach.
He is a great house seen from afar.
     no multitude can plunder it
          but if they do   it takes revenge
and when those from oversea catch sight of him
     they become his servants.
Ibonia is a bull   whose horns curve forward
     dangerous to fight him.
What is caught on his horns   is pierced
     those fixed by his glance   go bald
what is on his ears   he shakes off
     what is on his tail   he switches off
          what is under his hoof   he tramples.
His breath changes into a waterspout
     his right hand   kills ten thousand
          his left hand   kills a thousand.
His heel flares up   touching the ground.
     Grass dries
          earth shakes
               villages burn.
His village smells of cattle
     its ground smells of rum
          pieces of meat in melted fat

Just one cup of Inabo's rum makes a thousand men drunk."
So spoke Ranakombe.   He named the baby.

Power

Now as Ibonia was stoking the blazing fire
   thunder fell on him a lightning bolt
    the rocks rumbled
     the earth rose and sank. And Ranakombe said
"Ibonia, what say you? This is the Tormentor Prince
   He points at the sky the earth flames up
    He points at what is far but not what is near
     Me he torments.
Whatever he demands he gets
   what is claimed from him is not taken
    only he can make the earth drunk.
Those who see him in the skies he adds to his servants
   those who malign him everywhere them he adds too.
'They think they will stop me
   but with one blow I will sweep them away.'
That is a formidable man on the earth" said Ranakombe.
      Then Ibonia said,

   "A proud ruler am I!"
Again he leapt out of the fire.
 Where he walked, the earth cracked
   the wind roared,
    the trees withered to their roots,
      all waters dried up,
and all the people around him in the fire were starving.
He touched his father and mother
   and the people who died at his birth.
    They all came back to life.

Stone Man Shakes

Just then Stone Man slumped down three times.
  The sky, where Sky-Lord is, whirled
   the earth shook

the day of the sacred bath lost its power

storms raged all winter

the springtime was too hot.

That was a formidable man.

For himself he made things hard

for others he made things easy

but he had come into his own.

All the waters of Middle-River began to dry up.

All things in the house of Stone Man began to crumble.

Three times was Stone Man thrown into the air

before he found his feet.

Rainstorms pelted down.

Then said the Prince with Big Ears [father of Stone Man]:

"Here is my royal oration. Here is what I have to say to you, people of Middle-River.

Planters   do your planting

set out all your growing things

your plants growing in water

your crops in the earth.

It is the new season."

"Ah!" said Stone Man.

"Father seems to have knowledge   but he does not know

he seems to have memory   but he does not remember.

The 'line for two' is not made by my foot

The 'line for four' is not made by my hand.

If you think I am one who knows   I do know

if you think I am one who remembers   I do remember.

This is not the growing season

for what will happen next year I see this year

and what will happen tomorrow I see today.

This, then, is the royal oration I give you   people of Middle-River.

This now is no lifegiving thunder

this is no time to plant.

This is a deadly time"   said Stone Man.

"So those who have animals fattened, kill them

those who have thin animals, trade them.

That man's charms come from his bath
 That baby is bathing in hot coals.
No sacrificirg cattle, no sacrificing chickens!
 He doesn't bathe in water others have used
      but in hot coals from the west.
And his dogs Arched-Back and Long-Paw,
      with them he whips bulls
           and cuts the throats of chickens"   said Stone Man.
He knew about the baby from Iliolava (he did not see the baby born, for
Ibonia was born at Iliolava).
"Stone Man's nose is swollen with anger.
      This Betsiboka [river] is so high
           it can never be crossed without a pirogue.
Two pigs run here and there on the ground
      the oxen are heavy as iron
        the cows have shining coats
           the calves are filling out
              the bulls are huge
      the leaves are thick on the trees
           the tsipolitra [herbs] are tangling
              the grass is drying up.
But I am a broadshouldered prince
      and my charms too are potent.
Someone wishes the death of this kingdcm
      yet the Prince of Big Ears will destroy him.
No rival of mine can be the death of this kingdom"   said Stone Man.
"When I was about to act, I was stopped by Father.
      I can detect the far off
           I can detect the near.
Water creatures are fearful of Stone Man;
      no warming in the sun for them
           and the top of the village is no place for plundering
              for fear of Stone Man."

He Refuses More Names

Now Ranakombe spoke mighty words to Ibonia   who was turning homewards.

"To strengthen this baby, I add to his names
　　　　the name Loin-Girder.
What a heavy one, that child.
　　I will call him Girds His Loins Like Father of Male Big Maned Cat
　　　　　Big Man Who Attacks Him Will Have Broken Loins
　　　　　　　and Swollen Chest.
At the end of the game he has the same number of pieces as at the start
　　　　and his loins are girded　　　　like someone exhausted.
　　　　　He is a tough one."

"O, I do not want that name, father"　　　　said Ibonia.
"That means girding oneself like a thief
　　　hastening to turn one's back
　　　　preparing to flee.
　That is not facing one's enemy, but acting like a coward.
　They scratch everything they meet
　　　rock
　　　　wood
　　　　They dash into caves to hide.
That is running away, father"　　　　said Ibonia.

"What a heavy one, that child!"　　　　said Ranakombe.
"I will call him Girds His Loins Like Male Big-Winged Kite.
　Gently he takes his prey
　　carries it off
　　　leaves nothing but the smell.
　He girds himself like a man
　　　who is not embarrassed in front of women
　　　　who seizes his prey not with hands　　but with claws.
　　　　　　He is a proud one on the earth."

"O, I do not want that one, father"　　　　said Ibonia.
"That means girding oneself like a man with clipped wings.
　He grasps his food with foul back paws."

"What a heavy one, that child!"　　　　said Ranakombe.
"I will call him Girds His Loins Like Prince Drenched Cuckoo.

He flies, but not high
    he goes, but not far
        he eats, but slowly.
He makes rum without a still
    he has a thousand thrones
        and a hundred silver needles.
He has eight thousand to fan him.
  Fatted oxen surrender to him without a rope
    bulls fall of themselves
           he swallows them without butchering them.
He awakes to the conch and falls asleep to beating drums.
    It is he who awakes the day to be day
      and knows night will be night."

"O, I do not want that one, father"   said Ibonia.
"That means girding oneself like a coward.
    He sets out but never goes far
      he walks   but dares not go alone
        he stops for breath behind every tree."

"What a heavy one, that child!"   said Ranakombe.
"I will call you Girds His Loins Like Smith of the Silver Gods.
  He sports with his loincloth like a man playing on the edge of a cliff
    his chest is the mirror of his stomach
      his sides are like clear water
        like rocks with water flowing over them
        his loins are like silver links
          his calves are like posts sanded smooth.
He is a thousand men in accord
    a hundred men united.
When he girds himself, it's like many men marching
    a thousand fighters and a hundred weavers.
But Ibonia's loincloth is not spoiled by unskilled girls
    only strong women can take hold of it,"   said Ranakombe
      trying to fasten Ibonia's loincloth.

"O, I do not want that one, father"   said Ibonia.

"Oh, that baby is one heavy one,"   said Ranakombe.

"I will call you Girds His Loins Like Handsome Gray-Eyed Man.
    His tongue challenges the wind
        his body is like ice.
  It takes a hundred men to bestride his loincloth.
    Earth has no animal so dangerous"   said Ranakombe.

"O, I do not want that one, father"   said Ibonia.
"He cannot smite to death
    he can be hacked down by anyone
        then he can hardly get up.
  Dangerous men he can't injure
    He throws stones behind him
        he kills by cheating,
          he does not throw stones like a man.
  So I won't have that one"   said Ibonia.

"Oh, that baby is one heavy one," said Ranakombe.
"But I will call you Girds His Loins Like Prince Friday's Hog.
  One end of his loincloth is frayed.
  Fenced in, he roots his way out
    his sides are fat
      he kicks the grass
The end of his loincloth bounces
    his eyes butt like horns,
      his ankles make their own path
        the very end of his loincloth wounds   like a pile of stones.
He is stubborn
  he is indomitable
    he is the slicer
      he is the cutter
His belly is inflated
  he is the prince of steam
    he is a deceiver
What he does not catch nobody knows
  what he does catch is swollen
    he causes a great wound
      as bad as a first wife with no recompense.

Those he does not catch he disdains
>for he has made them jump
>>those he has touched with his foreigner's scissors
>>and those he has not caught
>>>will rue the day"   said Ranakombe.
"He is a formidable man on the earth, my boy"   said Ranakombe.
"Girding yourself like him is terrible, my boy."

"I do not want that one, father," said Ibonia.
"That's how a landless man girds himself.
 Such a king cannot rule
>the people cannot respect him
>>he cannot succeed his father
>>>he cannot keep his own heritage.
 He has no abode
>he hunts in the night of sleep time
>>and waits till day to sleep.
With no ricefield inherited, he has to depend on thievery instead
>His provisions for a journey are bitter herbs."

"Oh, that baby is one heavy one"   said Ranakombe.
"But I will call him Girds His Loins Like Manly Princess.
 The rear end of his loincloth drags on the ground
>the front end he plays with.
 It wraps him in silver
>wraps his loins in gold.
 He girds himself to dance all night
>and is girded for eight months.
 He governs the path of the sun
>working with one hand, then the other
>>day doesn't have to break for him
>>>nor sun to set without returning.
 A thousand men sing his praises
>ten thousand men serve him
 No bad man will meet him
>lazy men do not joke with him.
 The earth he has trodden is ruined and good for nothing.

His eyes are fierce
>   his forehead like the new moon
>   his teeth   smoothly planed posts
>   his calves   two meteors fallen to earth
>   his feet   spades pulled out of the ground
>   graceful is his pace.
> Rasoa   is the one he holds dear
>   too bad for those he doesn't."

That was the end of the duel of words between Ibonia and Ranakombe.

Ranakombe went back to his own village, and Ibonia stayed with his parents.

Games

There were four women, slaves of Great King-Maker, who had given birth at the same time as Rasoa. All four of the slave women's children were boys. So Great King-Maker gave them to Ibonia, and the slave boys grew up with Ibonia and played with him. When the five boys were grown, they went to play with the other children in the fields. That was where boys would throw clods of dung at each other. They split up into two teams — but Ibonia would not do that. He said, "All of you be one team, the five of us be the other." All the other boys said, "You can't do that, there's too few of you." (There were a good many children at Iliolava.) But Ibonia would not listen; he said, "Just go over there to that side. We will be the other team." Then they started throwing the manure. The boys Ibonia hit fell to the ground, and the ones he did not hit were dizzy and reeling. So the five slaves beat all the other boys.

That evening the boys went back to the village and said to their parents, "We fought with Ibonia with cowpats. It was just him and his four slaves on one team and all of us boys from Iliolava on the other team, but all of us could not win." And their parents said, "That's how weak you are. Five boys beating all the boys in Iliolava?"

Another day, Ibonia played again with the boys in the fields, throwing mud at each other. The same five were one team, and the other boys did not win. That evening they went to their parents and said, "We got beaten by those five slaves." And their parents said, "It's as if you didn't get enough to eat, if five people can beat you." So the boys said, "Then you go to the fields when Inabo [Ibonia] goes to the fields." Then one day Ibonia went to the fields with the boys, and they were throwing clods of earth, but the boys did not win. And the adults who had come there to watch were surprised to see the clouds of dust Ibonia threw up.

Later, they were throwing rocks, and again Ibonia was the winner. Still later, all the young men of Iliolava played there in the field with Ibonia and his five slaves. They did arm-wrestling and boxing. Later they did jumping. Some tried hard and did two lengths, some did two and a half lengths, some did three. Finally Ibonia too tried, and he jumped over a hill that was three days' march away. When the young men reached the village, they went to the villagers and said, "We did jumping with Ibonia. He went last. He jumped over that hill over there, and jumped over some others too, and we do not know how far he has gone." People were surprised to hear that, and said, "Bad news for us if the king's son is lost or dead." But when his parents heard about it, they did not worry. They knew their son. And when three days passed, Ibonia showed up. (He came all the way back on foot, and did not jump.)

Once Ibonia was grown up, he did not play in the fields with boys any more. He changed the names of the slaves with him, as they were all grown up too. His favorite he called Goodlooking; another he called Handsome Lad Doesn't Work, another Seldom Goes to the Fields, and another Likes Rice Water.

Ibonia sat playing *fanorona* at the gate with his mother's sister.[23] It was spring. And Ibonia said,

> "O Other-Mother!
>> The days are hurrying toward spring
>>> the workers are tilling the fields
>>>> I long for my betrothed."

Other-Mother said, "Hush, child. You're only a boy; you have palms like a woman.

>> Stone Man is a meteor
>>> Stone Man is a thunderbolt."

"Oh, Other-Mother," said Ibonia,

>> "I am tender with you, yes,
>>> but may others know how tough I am.

---

23 *Fanorona* is the Malagasy board game, historically symbolizing strategy on the battlefield.

A big building seen from afar am I
 a whole crowd cannot crack it
  but if they do, it takes revenge."
Then Goodlooking said,
"Make your own way, cousin
 make your own way, cousin.
You are a child of the moon
 a grandchild of the sun
  high in the sky.
You are a child of one who not in mockery is named Prince
 for you are a son of Prince Alone
  a grandson of Him Whose Memory Withers Not.
Blessed and shining may you be in Iliolava."

     "Yes,"   said Ibonia.
"I stand up the sky breaks
 I bend my head the earth breaks
  I lean over the eastern forest burns
   I kick the earth in Iliolava it dissolves in mud."

And Ibonia made the earth shake with his foot. It trembled and shook as far away as Many-Palms, where Stone Man lived. Things there fell off the shelves. Then Stone Man said,

"I do not see how this land of Many Palms will finish.
 It is to be conquered by a man with powerful charms.
So those who have animals fattened kill them
 those with thin animals trade them."

His father, Prince of Big Ears, said to him, "That is only your fear. How can this land be conquered by one man with powerful charms?"

        "Ah," said Stone Man,
"Father seems to have knowledge but does not know,
 he seems to have memory but does not remember." Stone Man
left off and said no more. He went off by himself, heavy-hearted.

Now Ibonia, in Iliolava, passed through the entry gate and went back to his house.

He Arms Himself

Another day, Ibonia and his mother's sister were playing *fanorona* in the house, and Ibonia said to her,

"I became betrothed when just conceived

I was married as a baby.

And if Girl of Grace dies

I will not leave her on the earth

if she lives, I give her to no man."

And Other-Mother said, "Hush, child. She is not the only wife for you." But Goodlooking then said,

"Make your own way, cousin

make your own way, cousin.

Blessed are you,   Ibonia

rich in goods   rich in property

without sin   without fault

an arum Iliolava loves to taste.

You will braid Many-Palms like a head of hair."

"I am a big man," said Ibonia.

"The name I will give this spear   which I will carry to fight Stone Man

will be Spear Many Trust

Spear Many Can Wield

Forged on Sunday

Bearded on Monday

Digs In Earth With Tenrecs,

Submerges in Water With Eels.

He is an edible arum in a rock cleft

not dug for the roots   not plucked for the leaves

if the wind does not behead it

it will not be pulled up."

Then he said,

"Yes, I am a big man.

The name of my axe will be

Male Iron Sparing No Shrub

Struck By Pirogue Not Turning

Delicious As Unique Lemon Grass

Does Not Chatter With Birds

Does Not Think With His Knees

Peerless Life   Protector Against Death."

Then he said,

"Yes, I am a big man.

The name of this knife of mine will be

Needs No Sambia [blade] To Cut

Needs No Axe To Slice

Grandson of the Long Streams

Needs Not Breed to Have Animals to Slaughter."

Then he said,

"Yes, I am a big man.

The name I will give this ox of mine will be

Born of Wild Silver

Smoking Firebrand

Firebrand of Perfumed Fire.

At command he goes in a circle

chewing, he is quiet

drinking, he 'takes all the pieces'

lying down, he casts a big shadow

eating, he swallows in one gulp

trampling, he beautifies the land.

He is victorious.

From him the people draw their strength."

He Is Tested

Now Ibonia went to Ranakombe's house. When he got there, Ranakombe was warming himself in the sun. Ranakombe said, "Now, what man is burning me?

Is it Male Cat With Big Nape?

Is it Manly Princess?

Is it Big Chameleon?

— the one who butchers what he will not cook

and cuts what is not eaten?

Is it the Prince Who Does Not Mix With Others?"

        But Ibonia said nothing.   Ranakombe said,

"This is Prince Beau-Regard, Prince Who Torments

        that slim peaceable man

            who needs war to fatten him.

If he makes war today   he is like a clod of earth

        but if he does not fight   he is as thin as a comb.

Pride swells him up

        submission emaciates him."

        Ibonia said, "Ah there, Other-Mother!"

"Where will you go now, Ibonia?"   said Ranakombe.   Ibonia said,

"It's not that misfortune has struck me, Ranakombe

        but here is what casts me down: my marriage.

My wife *Iampelasoamananoro* [Girl of Grace] has been stolen

        by that scourge   that disaster.

        I am going to bring her back.

I became betrothed when just conceived

        I was married as a baby.

        Dead   I will not leave her in the earth

        alive   I give her to no man."

        Then Ranakombe answered, in prophecies as usual:

"Go you to that forest in the east

        lead a plain red ox

            go into the forest.

If swine bar your way   do not go on

        but if kestrels bar your way   then go on.

You will hear all the trees in the forest speaking. They will say

        'I am Single Trunk

            I am Enough To Fill The Earth

                I am Red Leafless.'   But you answer them

'No, you are not. You are an impostor.'

When you have reached Red Leafless

        — they make talismans out of it —

there will be a waterspout

        but it will not speak. So you speak, and say

'If you are Single Trunk

Enough To Fill The Earth
        Red Leafless
  then stop the wind
        and take down this ox without a rope
                and light the fire to roast the ox.
    Then stretch out into a chain
        and hang on me
                if you are of any use.'
  When that is done," said Ranakombe
            "and when all you have ordered is accomplished
                    then go to the water's edge.
    As the sun is setting
            dive into the water with your talismans.
  If till daylight you can stay under water without coming up
                then you will get Girl of Grace [*Iampelasoamananoro*] as your wife.
  But if you cannot pass this test, then do not go
            for you will not get her
                    and Stone Man will kill you."
  So Ibonia set out, leading the ox with a plain red hide.
  When he reached the mouth of the forest, he said
  "If what I mean to do be not good for me
            may a hog go at me
    but if it be only good for me
            may a kestrelhawk rush upon me."
    And just then a kestrelhawk came in his way.
  When he entered the forest   the trees spoke.
  One said, "I am Red Leafless"
            another said, "I am Enough To Fill The Earth"
                    another one said, "I am Single Trunk."   And Ibonia said,
  "No, you are not. You are an impostor."
  And when Ibonia reached Red Leafless
            wind began to blow
                    trees began to twist.   Ibonia spoke, saying
  "If you are Single Trunk
            and Enough To Fill The Earth
                    and Red Leafless

> then stop the wind
>> take down this ox without a rope
>> and light a fire to roast the ox.
> Then stretch out into a chain   and hang on me.
> And if this journey is benign and auspicious for me
>> then I order you to stuff the ox
>>> with the leaves left over from your stretching."
> And the leaves left over from the stretching filled the ox's belly.

> He also said

> "If all is benign and auspicious for me
>> may the leaves return where they were."
> And the charms accomplished everything Ibonia commanded.

Then Ibonia went to the water's edge and waited for the sun to go down. As the sun was going down, he too went down into the water, with his talismans. He managed to stay there until daybreak before he came up. Then he went back to Iliolava.

He Combats Beast and Man

When he got there, he stopped at the entry gate, as before. He dug into the dry earth and buried himself up to his armpits. People were coming out and going in to the village with their things — water jugs, rice, firewood —but he would stab everything with his spear, and it all fell into the ditch. (Living beings he did not stab.) So people went to Great King-Maker and Rasoa and said, "Ibonia is at the entry gate, playing games with people. Going out or in, he stabs all their bundles with his spear, so that they all fall into the ditch."

When he heard that, Great King-Maker said to Rasoa, "That son of yours, Rasoa! If I go out there, I will kill that son of yours." But Rasoa said, "Now really, Great King-Maker! He was not born from me alone, he was born of both of us. If you [can] kill him, it brings no curse."

Great King-Maker went out and said, "Come together, Iliolava!" The people assembled. Great King-Maker ordered them to gather stones and pelt Ibonia. But they could not get anywhere near Ibonia. When they did, he would stab them with his spear. The people stoned him but did not hit him, though they threw stones that would make a *tatao* [mound]. (It's said that that was how the *tatao* cult began.) Then the people and Great King-Maker went back in; they never hit him.

Rasoa then came out into the public square, shaking her head, and went up to the entry gate, acting haughty and proud. She said,   "What is all this, Ibonia?

Are you wicked?
    Are you cowardly?
Are you acting like Blunderer's bull?
    shout at him   he does not roar
        prod him   he does not fight
            butcher him   his meat is not tender
Or like a cow whose milk is unfit to drink?
    What to do?
As if we were fighting rams:
    shout at them   they do not pull
        leave them alone   they break their heads.
I will not have it, you *Ingolimby* [Dullard]!
If Ibonia is truly strong
    isn't there a big crocodile there to the north
        killing off cattle and the people passing by?
If Ibonia is really a man, go there and fight it."

Ibonia came out of the earth, saying, "I am proud!
 With you I am gentle
    but with others I am tough.
 I am the kite's claws
    the eagle's talons
what I'm not offered   I take
    what I'm offered   I took already
        what I grab does not escape."

Then he called Goodlooking, Handsome Lad Doesn't Work, Seldom Goes to the Fields, and Likes Rice Water, and said, "Braid me a rope. I will fight that crocodile to the north."

He went to the water's edge, tied the rope under his arms, and declared

"If you see blood upstream
    pull me out, because I have been killed by the crocodile;
 if you see blood downstream
    then pull, because I have killed the crocodile."

Then he dived into the water and the crocodile snatched him. They fought there about three rice-cooking-times. Then he killed the crocodile. They saw the blood downstream. His four men were glad. They quickly pulled the rope to give the signal. Then they pulled Ibonia out, and the crocodile too. Then the four of them said,

> "Powerful is our father
> > powerful is our father.
> Ibonia is a thunderbolt,
> > our lord is a meteor,
> > > he is not a human being."

The villagers were glad that the crocodile was dead. It had been devouring everything that passed by.

Then Ibonia and his slaves returned and again placed themselves at the entry gate. They played the same game with the villagers, stabbing people's bundles just as before. Then Great King-Maker said to Rasoa, "That baby of yours, Rasoa! If I go out there, I will kill that baby." And Rasoa answered as she did before. So Great King-Maker called for spears and ordered them to be thrown at Ibonia. But again they could not hit him, because he turned the spears away with his magic wand, *kiabaly*; he was not touched. When they had done that, Great King-Maker and the rest came wearily back.

Then Rasoa came out again and acted the same as before, saying, "Truly, Ibonia, you are either wicked or cowardly. If you are really strong, then go and fight Savage Bull. He is the strongest animal. Go out and fight him, if you are so strong."

> Ibonia said, "I am made by power.
> With you I am gentle, but with others I am tough.
> As for Savage Bull
> under his hoofs I will not be trampled
> > under his thighs I will not be kicked
> > > on his lower jaw I will not be chewed
> even on the point of his horns   I
> > I will not be gored.
> Firstborn am I upon the earth."

Then he came out, called his four slaves, and set out for the place where Savage Bull was. When they reached there, he ordered the slaves to call Savage Bull. They said, "How do we call him?" Ibonia said, "Call like this:

'Aay, Savage Bull!

Aay, Savage Bull!

Get over here!

The one to fight you has come!'"

The slaves called him like that. When Savage Bull heard the call, he came near. His breath raised whirlwinds as he looked round to fight Ibonia. When he came to where Ibonia was, Ibonia touched his forehead with the *kilangaly* [wand]; he did not gore him. Then he bit Ibonia, but he did not bite down. He had to swallow him whole. Ibonia came out at his tail end. Then Savage Bull trampled him, but did not make mud of him. Again he swallowed Ibonia, who tore out Savage Bull's vital organs, and he died. Then Ibonia took his horns back to Iliolava.

Then Ibonia again placed himself at the entry gate, and he stabbed people's bundles as he had done before. The people again told Great King-Maker about it; he sent out Rasoa as before, and she too did just as she had done. Then Great King-Maker called for guns and had them fired at Ibonia, but they did not hit him.

Rasoa came out then and said, "If you are so strong, Ibonia

go out to Big Chameleon Man

he butchers what is not to be eaten

he chops up what is not to cook."   Ibonia said,

"I am made by power

I am Enough to Fill the Earth.

A lily on the water am I

set afire, I do not burn

burned, I do not burn up.

A nettle on high ground am I

killed, I do not die

burned, I do not burn up.

Though cursed to death

I am just beginning to live.

What I fix in place does not move."

He led his four servants to where Big Chameleon Man was. They found him catching wild cattle. He said to his servant Goodlooking, "Call out, Goodlooking, and say, 'Who is this who is hunting Ibonia's cattle?'" Goodlooking repeated Ibonia's words in a great shout. When Big Chameleon Man heard that, he said to his fellows, "Be quiet, you lot!" Ibonia said again,

"Call again. He is listening." Then Goodlooking called again, "Do not hunt the cattle of Ibonia, I say!"

Big Chameleon Man answered, "The cattle of Rasoalao have no owner.[24] The strongest man is their owner."

Ibonia called back, "Rasoalao does not own them, Ibonia does. But what does Big Chameleon Man want of me, that he comes quarreling?"

Big Chameleon Man said, "No. Ibonia does not own them, Rasoalao does. But if Ibonia wants to fight with me, let him come out and fight.

Maybe Ibonia does not know Big Chameleon Man,

who butchers what can't be eaten,

and chops up what can't be cooked."   Ibonia answered,

"I am Enough to Fill the Earth.

I am a teal on the water

set afire, I do not burn

burned, I do not burn up.

I am a nettle on high ground

killed, I do not die

burned, I do not burn up.

Though cursed to death

I am just beginning to live.

What I fix in place does not move."

The two men then shot at each other, but neither was wounded, only their clothes were torn. Then they fought with spears, but neither was wounded. Then they did arm wrestling, each one beat the other to the ground. When Big Chameleon Man hit Ibonia, he pushed him in up to his knees. Ibonia got up and hit Big Chameleon Man; he went in up to his armpits. Then Big Chameleon Man said, "Very well, Ibonia. Count me among your servants." So he was beaten.

Then Ibonia again placed himself at the entry gate and did the same thing, stabbing people's bundles as he had done before. Again the people told Great King-Maker and Rasoa about it, as they had done before. And Great King-Maker said to Rasoa, "That baby of yours, Rasoa! He has not changed. But if I go out there — well, I have waited till now, but this time I will kill him." Rasoa said, "Do as you must, Great King-Maker. If now

---

24 Wild cattle are said to be owned by Rasoalao (Ra-shoo-a-la-oh), the mythical wife of the giant Rapeto.

he is killed by you his father, it brings no curse. He is 'a crocodile baby, swallowed by its mother, devoured by the belly that carried him.'"

Great King-Maker went out again and called the people of Iliolava. When the people had assembled, he said, "Fire the cannon at him." They fired the cannon, but did not hit him. When the smoke of the cannon cleared away, they saw Ibonia — not dead, not wounded, but alive. After that the gunners got tired, and with Great King-Maker they went back in.

Then Rasoa again came out into the public square and went up to the entry gate, acting haughty and proud. She said,

> "Ibonia, you are bad, you are cowardly.
>
> You act like Imozy's bull
>
> > shout at him, he does not roar
> >
> > > prod him, he does not fight
> > >
> > > > butcher him, his meat is not tender.[25]

Ibonia, if you are so strong, go to where Manly Princess is. She is a strong one." Ibonia said,

> "I am made by power.
> > With you I am gentle, but with others I am tough."

And then he went to where Manly Princess was. Again he took his four slaves with him, and five bulls and some provisions. When they reached the village of Manly Princess, no one was there. When they saw no one there and an empty village, Ibonia said to his servants, "Where are these people gone, men? All the furnishings of the houses are still here, but the people are not." Then he said to one of his servants, "Stay here, my man, kill an ox, have it ready when we come back. We'll go find out where the villagers have gone."

As the slave was cooking and roasting the meat, it gave off a charred smell. Then a large animal came out of the water into the village. It meant to eat the one slave left there and the meal he had prepared. It was this animal that had eaten the people of the village and every living thing it found. But Ibonia was far away. When the slave saw the animal, he fled. The animal was the size of a mountain. The slave peeped through a hole at the animal, and there he was, eating the meat. He was frightened and wondered what he would say to Ibonia. He said to himself, "If I tell Ibonia

---

25   Whether Imozy (Mr. Clumsy) is a proverbial name or not, her indirect slam at Ibonia is cast in perfect proverbial rhythm, like many other epithets in the poem.

about this, he will fight the animal and kill it. But if I don't tell him, then he will not leave me alone until I tell him where the meat is gone. Well, I won't tell him. He will do what he will do."

When Ibonia came, he said, "Bring on the food." And the slave said, "I left it. I had to run after the cattle. I did not see what ate it." Ibonia was angry and said, "Now I see what my father told me: 'They cannot take care of you, Ibonia; take more people with you.'"

Next day he left another slave there. He again ordered him to kill an ox, but that animal ate it up like the other one. He had all four men take turns; then only one ox was left. Ibonia said, "Go you and look for those people. I will be the one to stay." The servants left, but they did not go far. They just peeped through, saying, "We'll be in trouble if the son dies. That animal is the one that has eaten the people of this place."

Ibonia killed the ox, cooked some of it on the fire, and roasted the rest. When the animal smelled the smell of char, it came up and said,

"Bring out what is cooked
cook what is raw.
I am here, the one it was made for."

Ibonia was startled, looked around, and jumped when he saw the animal. Then he said to his talismans,

"What to do, O Resolute?
O Enough to Fill the Earth?
O All Raw?
If I go forward, I will be conquered by this creature.
If I go back, I will be disgraced before my father."[26]

The talismans trembled. He put the skewer on the fire. The animal got jumpy. It said, "Draw back! In one gulp I have swallowed thousands upon thousands of people and thousands upon thousands of cattle, and you, all alone, are blocking me?" Ibonia went on heating the skewer. When the animal was about to swallow him, he threw the iron into its mouth. The animal roared, the iron made a great noise in its mouth. It would not come out. The animal died. Then Ibonia unstitched its belly, and there were all the

---

26 Contrast Ibonia's victory over the dilemma with the guineafowl who in a Merina tale falls and breaks a wing in the forest, originating the proverbial saying, "Guineafowl in the middle of the forest: go forward, he can't; go back, wing broken; stay there, longs for his relatives" (Dahle 298).

people and living things the animal had swallowed. They were all still alive, not one dead, but every one of them was thin; all thin. And Ibonia brought all those people and living things back to life, and they were all alive.

Then Manly Princess and her people said, "We were dead and now are living. Ibonia, from now on I am your child, and I obey you. From now on, you are lord and ruler of this land." But Ibonia refused, saying, "Be your own lord and ruler. I must still rescue Girl of Grace. But I tell you just this: go to another place. That monster may have friends." And the people did go to another place.

He Refuses Other Wives

When Ibonia came back, he did not place himself at the entry gate of Iliolava. His father and mother were glad of that. Ibonia said,

"The baby is not mad
	the season is no empty boast.
  Now it is spring
	  people are digging the fields.
	But Ibonia is longing for Girl of Grace." Rasoa said,
"O Ibonia, you have hands like a baby's
	hands like a woman's.
 You will not be able to stand the blows of Stone Man.
	Stone Man is a thunderbolt, a meteor.
	  His fingers are horns
		he uses his fists like hammers
			his head he uses as an anvil." But Ibonia answered,
"I became betrothed when just conceived
	I was married when still a baby.
 If Girl of Grace dies
	I will not leave her in the earth,
 if she lives
	I give her to no man.
 I will give her to no one. She is my wife."

Then Rasoa replied, "Enough, Ibonia. If you are really in search of a wife, there is the daughter of the Prince of the West. She is noble."[27] He said yes.

---

27   "Although Ibonia is his father's murderer (one does not know exactly how), his affection

They sent for that girl, and she came. Then said Ibonia,

"Send that girl back.

  She has bushy eyebrows.

    She is one of those who cast the evil eye at their husbands

      as [soon as] they set up house.

Still —   she is beautiful among the beautiful,

      good among the good

        so give her money   give her precious stones."

Then they brought him the daughter of the Prince of the South. When she came, Ibonia said,

"She is beautiful among the beautiful

      good among the good.

Yet she has one small fault —

      her feet are cracked.

  She is a carrier of ulcerous disease

      she will bring sand into the bed.

With those long nails

      she will never be a basket-weaver.

  So send the girl back,

      but give her money   give her precious stones."

Then Andriantsifamaho [Lord Not to Be Mixed With], who was Ibonia's mother's brother, heard about this. He lived in Imanambaho. He said to his slave, "Zealous One, go to Iliolava and say to Great King-Maker, Rasoa, and Ibonia,

'If it is a wife you want, Ibonia, your uncle's daughter is noble, she is a queen.

    Her mirror is a golden mirror; her hairbrush is silver.

      When she goes, she is like a dance of warriors

        when she comes, she is like a line of dancers.'"

When Ibonia heard that, he answered, "This is my message to you, O messenger from Andriantsifamaho; tell him this:

'I will pull you out of bed

---

for his mother never falters and is an index of the profound identity of nature that quite obviously exists between a mother and a son when they face the same trials" (Ottino "Mythology of the Highlands" 964).

I will knock you on the hearthstones
> I will throw you down by the door
>> I will toss you in the ditch.'

Say that. If my uncle accepts that, then I will not fight. My wife can belong to Stone Man, and the daughter of Andriantsifamaho will be my wife. Also tell him,

'I will set his house afire, his village too
> but he will take nothing with him.
I will behead his children
> and hang their heads at the entry gate.
Kestrelhawks will perch there
> lemurs will feed on them.'

If Uncle accepts that, I will not fight. My wife can belong to Stone Man, and the daughter of Lord-Not-To-Be-Mixed-With will be my wife."

When Andriantsifamaho heard that, he was angry. He said,

"Let him go after whoever he wants
> let him fight as much as he wants.
>> A son-in-law of mine should be champion."

Then Ibonia said to Rasoa,

"A man who goes in quest of a wife can be killed. Let me go rescue Girl of Grace.

Plant this banana-tree now, and water it often.
> If it withers, I am sick,
>> if it dies, I too am dead,
>>> if it is green, then I too am healthy.
I will go leaping over the hills.
> Where I hit the ground   it dissolves in mud.
Where I kick the rocks   they roll like mountain torrents."

The Disguised Flayer

Then he set out, leaping, and he reached the Mananivo river [Many Palms]. The crocodile there said to him, "Are you so tired of living, or worn out with sighing, that you come here? Yesterday a hundred cattle and a thousand men tried to cross here and could not. And you alone want to cross here?"

And Ibonia said, "I am going to cross." He jumped in. The crocodile caught him; he hit the crocodile with the back of his hand. Then the crocodile said, "Very well, get on my back." Ibonia got up on the crocodile's back, and when they had gone some way, the crocodile said, "My part ends here, Ibonia. The rest is up to the shark." Ibonia left him.

The shark came along and said, "You will not cross here. Yesterday a hundred cattle and a thousand men tried to cross here and could not. And you alone want to cross here?" And Ibonia said, "To cross, yes." The shark came to seize him, but quickly he jumped on to the shark's back and broke his bones. The shark said, "Very well, get on my back." And all the water creatures did the same, so that Ibonia did cross the Mananivo ford.

Ibonia did not go directly into the village. Instead he went to look for Old Man, who was the keeper of Stone Man's fields. There was a well in the field, with a big rock; Ibonia climbed up on it. Old Man came to draw water. Looking into the water in the well, Old Man saw Ibonia's face in the water, but did not see his body up on the rock. Then Old Man said, "I look so fine. Should I be drawing water?" Then, it is said, Old Man broke the water jug and left, going back to his house. There he took a mirror and looked in it. But what he saw was different, not what he saw in the water.

Old Man went back to the well and looked around. He saw Ibonia up on the rock and said, "You are looking for trouble. What are you doing here, my lord? Stone Man does not like good people. He is envious and kills them all, the good people who come to Mananivo."

"Yes, father, but you and I can talk like family," said Ibonia. "How many wives has Stone Man?"

Old Man said, "There is Not Untouched by the Shrimp

No Prisoner of Day

Silver Stripe

Forged One

Fern Shoot

and Girl of Grace [Iampelasoamananoro]."

Ibonia said, "Which one is Stone Man's favorite?"

Old Man said, "He likes each and every one, but it is Girl of Grace he loves best."

So Ibonia said, "When you go to visit the prince, Old Man, what do you carry with you?"

Old Man answered, "What should I take, grandchild, but ripe bananas, seeds for herbs, herbs, citrus plants, and other little things?"

Ibonia said, "What is the first place you go when you get there?"

Old Man said, "To the east of the open space, to the house of Handsome-Gray-Eyed-Man."

Ibonia said, "Which house does he sleep in at night, Old Man?"

Old Man answered, "East of the open space, at Girl of Grace's house. He goes there to sleep because he gets sweet food and choice dishes."

Ibonia said, "Old Man, let us go like kinsmen to your house and prepare some food."

Old Man said, "Come along." And like a son [following Ibonia] he started for Old Man's house. Ibonia said, "You go first, Old Man." And Old Man went first, while Ibonia watched his way of walking. When he caught on to Old Man's walk, he seized Old Man by the hair (it is said), he struck him down, he threw away his bones and flesh, and he took his skin to dress in.

An Old Man Becomes Stone Man's Rival

Then Ibonia picked some ripe fruits in the fields, to take to Mananivo village and to offer to Handsome Gray-Eyed Man, Stone Man's father, and to Stone Man. He set out carrying the fruits and herbs on his shoulders, disguised as Old Man. Stone Man's talismans shook and said, "Your rival is coming. He cares for nothing." Then Ibonia came and entered the royal compound. The young princesses and Handsome were surprised. Handsome said, "Here comes a slave from old days." He put down the things he had brought, to the south of the hearth. The young princesses bickered over the fruits.

That evening, Handsome said, "Where are you going to sleep, Old Man?" Old Man said, "In the house where I always sleep, of course, with the dear child Girl of Grace. The plate I eat from is there, the spoon I eat with is there, the mat I lie on is there." So he went to Girl of Grace's house.

When the rice was cooked, it was put in front of him, in his usual dish. The dish cracked; the spoon broke. Girl of Grace was angry at her servants, and said, "What do you have against Old Man, that you broke his plate and spilled his rice?" Then Girl of Grace put her own dish of rice in front of him. When Old Man was about to lie down, they unrolled the sleeping mat he always used. It shredded into small pieces. Again Girl of Grace was angry, and said, "Your hands are too rough. Mats do not shred for no reason. You are doing him harm." She ordered another mat brought for him.

Morning to night, Stone Man's talismans kept saying, "Your rival is coming. He cares for nothing. Your rival is coming. He cares for nothing."

Next morning, Handsome and Stone Man were playing *fanorona*. Old Man came up and said, "I used to play that with your grandfather. Let me do it now; I used to, but not any more." He stood beside Handsome. He looked at the board and then said, "I see it now, my lord, and I will 'kill' [checkmate]." Stone Man said, "Do it then. Let's see if you 'kill' me." And when he advanced his pieces, he "killed" Stone Man. They divided the pieces again, and Stone Man got killed three times, four times. Then Stone Man became angry and said, "Aah, father, this is not Old Man. If it is, how does he know how to play *fanorona*? His job is weeding the fields. Let me shoot him with my gun, father," he said. "This is a different Old Man."

Handsome said, "Now look! Am I going to let the slaves of my ancestors be massacred? Wait until Friday. Thursday is still my day. I will not allow any slave of my ancestors to be shot with a gun. That man played *fanorona* with my grandfather and my father. Now he is teaching you something, and as soon as he 'kills' you you want to kill him! If you want to play the fool, my son, you will really be doing that if you kill the slaves of my ancestors." Stone Man could not overcome the stubbornness of Handsome. He left and went back to his house.

The next day, Stone Man was playing with the young men in Many-Palms. They played cross-sticks.[28] The boys gathered into two teams. When one team attacked Stone Man, he caught all the crosses they threw. When it was Stone Man's turn to throw, the ground where the crosses passed over caught fire, and none of them could be caught. Old Man, who was looking on at Handsome's side, said, "Allow me to 'let go of my soul' [prepare for death], Handsome. I cannot look on at these boys' games any longer." But Handsome stopped him, saying, "Don't do it. Stone Man will kill you. Maybe you did not see: when you beat him at *fanorona*, he almost murdered you." Old Man said, "What is it to you if I am killed by my own son? Let me go and do it, to 'let go of my soul'."

Old Man strode over there and said, "Let me play with you, boys. I've watched your game, I am ready to prepare for death. This takes me back to what we used to do back then." And Stone Man said, "Let him do it, this disgusting fellow, so I can kill him." Old Man did not go to Stone Man's

---

28 A game in which a star made of wood is thrown back and forth (Decary *Moeurs et coutumes* 170).

team; he went to the other team. And it was him that Stone Man aimed at with his cross-stick. Stone Man said,

"This cross-stick, this is me, Stone Man.
It touches only the top of the forehead,
it does not go out except through the heart.
What it hits   it kills,
what it does not hit   it makes dizzy."

He threw his cross-stick at Old Man; it started a fire as it went by. But Old Man easily caught the cross-stick which Stone Man threw and held on to it. Then it was Old Man's turn to throw, and he said,

"This cross-stick, this is me, Old Man.
If Stone Man does not catch it, he will be dizzy.
If he does catch it, he will be carried into the air
and his body will be bruised."

Then Old Man threw the cross-stick. Stone Man just caught it, but it knocked him down and his knees, elbows and sides got bruised. Then Stone Man tried again, but Old Man made an easy catch. Everyone was surprised. Then the cross-stick players divided up. Stone Man was angry again, because people were talking about Old Man winning, saying, "Stone Man could not beat Old Man." Stone Man said to his father, "Enough, father. I will kill that Old Man, because that is not Old Man, it is someone else. If it were Old Man, could he beat me? What is he but an old man?" But Handsome did not agree to that.

The next day, Stone Man again called the boys of Many-Palms, and ordered them to drive in the strongest oxen, to soften the fields. "Today we will do our planting," he said. When the strong oxen were in, they did the softening. Old Man followed Handsome to watch the tramplers. Then the boys took the oxen by the horns; some of them Stone Man slapped, and those ones got flayed. So the oxen charged, galloping into the ricefields. Old Man said to Handsome, "Prince, I'll go along and soften the fields." Handsome tried to stop him, but he was not willing and went down anyway to trample. "I cannot stand it any longer, Prince, watching Prince's boys grabbing the oxen," said Old Man. And when Stone Man saw that Old Man had gone down there, he said, "This time I'm going to kill that wildcat." When Old Man was right in the middle of the ricefield, Stone Man turned his oxen around to face him. He slapped them, and they galloped up on Old Man to tread him down. But Old Man seized the cows and used them to club the oxen, and the oxen died. And he clubbed the bulls with the oxen, and the bulls died. And he clubbed the young oxen with the bulls, and the young oxen died too. Then Stone Man became angry, as before, because many of his cattle were dead. Again he wanted to kill Old Man, but Handsome did not allow him to. And the tramplers went back to the village.

Now Old Man transformed himself into a *papango* [yellow-billed kite], to go after Stone Man's talismans — the ones named Unseen Body, Continuous Murmur, and Great Burning Fire. But he did not find them. Then he transformed into a cat; still he could not find them. And he transformed into several other things; still he did not find those talismans belonging to Stone Man. At last, to find Stone Man's talismans he transformed into wind. Then he did find Stone Man's talismans. He polluted them and destroyed them so as to put an end to their power.

Now, they say, trouble came upon Stone Man. He called the people of Many-Palms saying,

> "Those who own lean animals   trade them
>   those who own fat animals   destroy them
>   for no one knows how this land of Many Palms will end.
>   The land will be conquered by a man
>   whose talismans are powerful
>   but who himself is a man of power."

Victory: "Dead, I Do Not Leave You on Earth; Living, I Give You to No Man"

When night came, Old Man went to his sleeping house, but Stone Man did not go to sleep there, because that was his day for a different wife. When the people in that house were fast asleep, Ibonia lit the fire. Then he took off the skin of Old Man, which he had been wearing. Girl of Grace started up, looked at the people in the house, and saw Ibonia. She said, "Ohh! Who are you? Why are you murdering yourself? — for you will surely die here, you will not live. Stone Man is a disaster man, a calamity man, a thorn it's better not to touch." Ibonia answered,

> "I am Ibonia!
>   The law of marriage lasts till death.
>   I pledged myself to you when I was just conceived

I married you as a baby.
  If you die
    I will not put you in the ground
  if you live
    I give you to no man."

Girl of Grace said, "Yes, Ibonia, so be it. May the morning not be the end of both our lives!" Then Ibonia played the *valiha* [stringed instrument]. The village people heard him, and in the morning they said, "That's someone else, someone else; that's not Old Man."

Then Stone Man, angry, tried to open the house but he could not. He set fire to the house but it would not burn. He tried to cut the cornerstones, but his ax bounced off and only got chipped. He dug the ground, but his spade was no use and it broke.

Then from outside the house he called:
"How will you steal my wife   here in Many-Palms
    if you stay in the house   and do not come out to fight?"
Ibonia, inside the house, answered, "That Stone Man,
    he is big   but he is cream
      he is fat   but he is milk.
        He will not resist Ibonia's blows.
  I the stranger rule the road
    Stone Man the owner retreats.
  I, Ibonia, the stranger
    am the one to sleep in this bed
      Stone Man, the owner, is the one to sleep on the ground."
            Stone Man answered:
"Ibonia has hands like a woman's
    but I gird myself like Big With Many Amulets
      I spend my time in secret.
  I am stronger than those from long ago
    but Ibonia is a runt
      he cannot resist my blows."
            Ibonia answered,
"As I climb a hill
    I get stronger and stronger
  as I come down the other side

I do not limp.
Where I walk turns into mud
   what I hit does not get away.
I am no banana-tree with a cluster on its top
   I am no sugarcane with big young leaves
      I am not rainwater that lasts all night
I am no mist covering the earth
   I am no swallowing crocodile lying at the ford
      I am no crocodile to bite those in the water.
I am descended from the great
   a child of those great in future and the great of old.
I stand up and the sky breaks
   I stoop and the earth breaks
      I lean over and the eastern forest burns
         I kick the earth of Many Palms   it dissolves in mud
         I am strongest of all."
Stone Man, outside the house, said,
   "I am one a thousand pirogues cannot stop.
      Those who ford, I chew up their loins,
         those who cross   I kill by thousands.
Why then does Ibonia stay in the house and not come out to fight?"

Then Ibonia had Girl of Grace dress in all her finery inside the house, before he would go out. When she finished adorning herself, they came out. Ibonia said,

   "When I swallow, there is much blood
      when I butcher, there are many guts.
   Cattle I drive can go the distance
      what Stone Man drives, no distance.
   The living belong to Ibonia
      the dead to Stone Man."

To Girl of Grace he said, "You stand at the window, and I will stand at the door." Girl of Grace said, "If I do not come out with you, I am dead." But Ibonia said, "As long as I am not dead, you are not dead."

Girl of Grace then went to the window, and Ibonia went to the door. They opened both together. Stone Man rushed upon Girl of Grace to stab her, but his spear deflected and stuck in the ground. Ibonia said,

"How will Stone Man be reputed a grown man

when he fights with women?

I am a man like him. Come out onto the ground for the match." The two men went out to the ground.

First they shot guns and threw spears; neither died. Next they beat each other on the dry ground. Ibonia got hit by Stone Man; he went in up to his knees. But he got free, and then he hit Stone Man, who sank in up to his thighs. Then Stone Man got free, and he hit Ibonia, who went in up to his armpits. "Aaay," said Ibonia to his talismans, "Completely Raw, Single Trunk, Leafless Red! Why did you not shame me in Iliolava, not confound me then, if you were going to let me fall here on the battlefield?" Then Ibonia used Stone Man like a sledgehammer; he sank in so deep that he disappeared. Ibonia filled in the hole.

Return of the Royal Couple

Then Ibonia said to Handsome and the people of Many-Palms, "Who will be your chief, the dead or the living?" Handsome said, "For us it is the living. Certainly the dead are no friends." That, they say, was the birth of the expression *Tsy maty ny namana*, 'There is no society with the dead.' So Ibonia said, "Be the ruler in your kingdom. I am returning to Iliolava, and I am taking Girl of Grace with me." And Ibonia started back to Iliolava; that was his country.

The banana tree Ibonia planted outside the house of Lady Beautiful-Rich was growing well. His mother drew hope from that and was glad: Her son was living, not dead at all.

When Ibonia and his wife were going to cross the Many-Palms river, Ibonia struck the water with his wand, saying,

"This water!

The top is not to sink

the bottom not to rise.

That water in the middle is to separate,

so Ibonia and his wife can cross."

Sand appeared, the waters separated. He and his wife went on the sand as if it were dry land. They reached Iliolava safe and sound. His mother and father and the people there were glad and made a great feast.

Ibonia Prescribes Laws and Bids Farewell

Ibonia and Girl of Grace stayed married about ten years. About three years before his death, he declared his will to his father and mother, his wife and children, and all the people in and around Iliolava. He said,

"This I declare to you: soon I am to return to the 'place of lying down.'

Close at hand is the day when Ibonia will be removed

and Inabo [another of his names] will go the way

of all those whose doors face west [the dead].

That is a fate that disheartens one's manhood. For to the earth we return.

Inabo is not of those who are buried to rot

he is of those who are planted to grow

dead by day, alive by night.

Inabo's return is coming.

These then are the orders I leave you.

First of things is marriage.

If you are a prince

if you are a ruler

if you are a governor

if you are a spokesman

do not untie the bonds of marriage!

The marriage tie is binding even unto death.

Do not divide it."

(This admonition, it is said, gave marriage the importance it has.)

"Second: listen. I shall change my name

for one's name on earth does not go back to heaven.

Before the lord of heaven all things are new.

My grandfather is holy.

These will be my names:

Lightning-Over-Half-the-Earth

Gashed-Earth

Thunderer-Heard-Afar.

Now listen, all of you.

When there is thunder

when the skies weep

when the rain falls

lament, O Beautiful-Rich,

>> for that will be your son,

>>> Thunderer-Heard-Afar."

(That, it is said, was the first time it was said, "It is a bad day for old women," when it thunders.)

And when the three years had passed — Ibonia had said, "I will die when three years have passed" — then he died.

Appendix: Versions and Variants

Comparison and Comparatism

Comparatism in folktale studies began by asking about the history of a folktale, viewing it as a thing, a cultural product. Where was the tale *Ibonia* born? How did it migrate? The answer comes when we put together its seemingly similar forms and look for common features and differences. In the past, it was assumed that most members of a folk group told pretty much the same tales in about the same way, and that the style was uniform for all members of a group. That assumption made it unlikely that collectors would look for variant forms of the same tale in the same community. The translations below disprove the old assumption; they are data for comparatism. It is easy enough to find similarities and differences; the challenge is to gather enough information to apply Kluckhohn's principle, that pre-existing cultural emphases govern the way a borrowed story is transformed.[29]

Text 0, Rasoanor. Antandroy, 1650s. The earliest published narrative anticipating *Ibonia*, from the survey of Madagascar by Étienne de Flacourt. He observed that the Antandroy performers used both speech and song, accompanying themselves on the *herranou*, a one-string instrument that was, in his time, the most widely heard instrument. Their repertoire, he says, comprised serious stories of past time [*angano*]; a performance might take a whole night to complete, sung without hesitation, with response especially from "all the women, who liked to sing. They could make a song out of any laughable action of a tale character." The *herranou* player

---

29   The original versions of many of the texts translated are available as supplementary
     material from the website associated with this volume
     http://www.openbookpublishers.com/isbn/9781909254053

                                                    DOI: 10.11647/OBP.0034.07

"tells his story in poetic terms [manner] quite pleasingly, and enlarges his story, which lasts a whole night". The story of Rasoanor reminded Flacourt of both the Biblical Jonah and Ovid's tale of Hero and Leander, but he conceded it was "in another fashion and quite different" (62–63).

Here is Flacourt's story.

This Rasoanor was the only son of a very powerful and rich king. His father wanted him to marry the daughter of another king, his neighbor, who was very beautiful. Rasoanor refused this match, and several others he was offered, because he was in love with the wife of a great lord, king of a faraway island, where she lived. He was so passionate about her that he considered having several large pirogues, or boats [*canots*], built to go and see this lord and offer him his services, so as to gain time to win the good grace of his mistress and wait for an opportunity to be able to take her away. His father, being warned of his scheme, did all he could to turn him away from it, advising him of the difficulty he would have in succeeding, the danger he was putting himself into if he was discovered, and the evil he would do by wanting to carry out such a pernicious scheme. He had his kinsmen and most trusted friends speak to him about it, he offered him other very advantageous matches; finally, as he could not win over his mind, he had all the boats broken up and burned, and forbade any to be made until his son would change his plan. Nevertheless Rasoanor kept to his intention, and when he saw he could have no boat, he said to his father that he would swim to the island where his dear mistress was. He warned his father and mother, all his beloved kinfolk, and all his father's subjects. He appointed the day, he came to the shore with a large crowd of people to see him off; he took his leave of his father and mother and all his kin, all tearful, and gave them hope that they would see him come back with his mistress. Threw himself into the sea, swam to where he was almost out of sight, a whale took him on her back, carried him for three months as far as that island, and gathered around her a great number of little fish, on which Rasoanor lived. He arrived at that island, where the lord of it received him cordially. For as much time as it took, he won the good graces of his mistress, took her away in a large pirogue with twenty slaves, who went with him to the shore of his own country, whence he had departed six months before, and was received with open arms by his parents.

Motifs: H1229, Quests voluntarily undertaken. T481, Adultery. R245, Whale boat. Cf. H1233.6.3 Porpoise as helper on quest. H1239, Accomplishment of quest.

Text 2, "Ibonia". Merina tale collected 1875–1877. From Vakinankaratra, the region of the plateau around Antsirabe and Betafo, south of Antananarivo. Dahle 155–163; Dahle-Sims 34–39. Translated by Rev. James Sibree, Jr. "Malagasy Folk-Tales" 49–55.

Once upon a time there were two sisters who had no children, and so they went to work the divination (*sikidy*) at the house of Ratobòboka. As soon as they came in she asked, "Why have you come here?" The sisters replied, "We are childless, and so have come to inquire by divination here of you". Then said Ratobòboka, "Look into my hair". So the elder one looked and saw only a bit of grass; then she said, "I saw nothing, mother, but this little bit of a red charm". Ratobòboka replied, "Give it me, for that is it". And upon this, Ratobòboka said, "Go alone to yonder forest to the east; and when you have arrived there the trees will all speak and say, 'I am the sacred child-charm'; but do not you speak for all that, but take the single tree which does not speak there, last of all, and take its root which lies to the east" So the two girls went away. And when they came to the forest each of the trees said, "I am a sacred child-charm" (*i.e.*, which causes the barren to bring forth). Nevertheless the sisters passed them all by. And when they came to the single one which did not speak, they dug round the tree, and saw one of the roots struck afterwards, which they thereupon took away.

And when they were on the road the sisters vowed, saying "If we should bear boy and girl (*i.e.*, if one have a boy and the other a girl), they shall marry each other". And when they came home they drank (of the charm). Accordingly the elder one became pregnant; and after a half-year had passed the younger also was with child. And when the time came for her to be delivered the elder sister bore a daughter, and she called its name Rasòamànanòro (or Rampélasòamànanòro). In due time came the day for her younger sister to be delivered, so she went to the south of the hearth to bring forth her child. But the child in her womb, they say, spoke and said, "I am not a slave, to be taken here south of the hearth"; so his mother went north of the hearth. Then it spoke again, "I am not a prince to be taken north of the hearth". Then his mother took him to the box but it said, "I do not like to be smoked". After some time, it said, "Make a big fire of wood". So they made it. Then it said again, "Swallow a knife for me, and take me west of the hearth". So he was taken there. And having come there, with the knife his mother had swallowed he ripped up his mother's womb, and then leaped into the fire which burned brightly there, after having patted the wound which he had made by ripping up his mother, so that it was healed. Then his father and mother endeavored to save him, lest he should be killed through going into the fire; but when they thrust out their hands to take him they were broken and unable to take hold of him; and so it happened with their feet as well.

And after a while the child spoke thus: "Give me a name". Then said his mother, "Perhaps you should be called Fòzanatokòndrilàhy, for I hear that he was a strong man". But the child did not like it; so his mother mentioned another name, and said, "Perhaps Ravàtovòlovoày then, for he, I understand, was famous for his strength". But he did not like that either. So the child gave himself a name, and said, "I am Ibonìamàsy, Iboniamanòro: breaking in pieces (*manòro*) the earth and the kingdom; at the point of its horns, not gored; beneath its hoofs, not trampled on; on its molar teeth, not crushed. Rising up, I break the heavens; and when I bow down the earth yawns open. My robe, when folded up, is but a span long; but when spread out it covers the heavens, and when it is shaken it is like the lightning. My loin-cloth, when rolled together, is but the size of a fist, but when unfolded it surrounds the ocean; its tongue (when girded) causes the dew to descend, and its tail sweeps away the rocks. Ah! I am indeed Ibonìamàsy, Iboniamanòro". And having spoken thus he came out from the fire and went upon his mother's lap.

And after he had grown up he had a dog called Rampèlamàhavàtra. One day while he was hunting in the fields, there came that famous man called Fòzanatokòndrilàhy to seek for Ibonia, and inquired of his parents, "Where is Ibonia?" They replied, "He has gone for pleasure into the forest". So he took Ibonia's dog, for the parents could not prevent it. And as soon as Ibonia returned from hunting he asked his parents, "Where has my dog gone?" They replied, "Fòzanatokòndrilàhy has taken him". So he said, "I am going to fetch my dog, father". But his father would not let him, for he said, "Why, child, even the crocodiles in the water are sought by Fòzanatokòndrilàhy, and found, and how can you fight with him without coming to harm?" But his father, seeing that he would not be warned, made him fetch a great stone, in order to see the strength of his son; then he said, "Since I can't persuade you, fetch me yonder big stone to make me a seat". So he went and fetched it. Then his father let him go. So off he went and came up with Fòzanatokòndrilàhy. And when the latter saw him he said, "What are you seeking for here?" Ibonia replied, "I want my dog". So he asked him, "Are you strong?" "Yes", replied Ibonia, "I am strong". And no sooner had he said so than Fòzanatokòndrilàhy seized him, and threw him more than the length of a house. And so they went on, first one and then the other, until each had thrown his opponent as far as ten house lengths. Then said Fòzanatokòndrilàhy, "Don't let us throw each other any more, but cast each other down" (a descent). So he lifted Ibonia up and cast him down, but he did not fall, but stuck in the ground as far as his ankles; then he, in turn, cast down Fòzanatokòndrilàhy, who descended as far as his knees. And so they went on with each other until Fòzanatokòndrilàhy was forced completely into the ground, that is, the rock on which they were contending, and Ibonia pressed down the stones upon him so that he was quite covered up.

Then Ibonia called together Fòzanatokòndrilàhy's subjects and asked them, "Will you obey the living, or the dead?" So his wife and people replied, "We will obey the living, sir". So they became Ibonia's subjects, and he departed with all his spoil.

And on his way back a number of people met him who were each skilled in various ways. Some were swimmers in deep waters, others were able to tie firmly, others again were able to see at great distances, others were able to make alive; and all these Ibonia showed kindness to, and gave them a share of the spoil which he had obtained. So he went on his way back and came to his village. Arriving there he could not find Rampélasòamànanòro, his betrothed wife, for she had been taken by Ravàtovolòvoay. So he asked his parents, "Where has my wife gone?" They replied, "She has been taken by Ravàtovolòvoay". So he said, "I am going to fetch my wife". When they heard that, his parents they warned him, saying, "Don't do that, child, for Ravàtovolòvoay is extremely powerful". But he would not stay. So at last his father got angry and took gun and spear to kill him, but he could do nothing to harm him, for the spear bent double when he hurled it. Upon that, Ibonia planted some arums and plantain-trees, and said to his parents, "If these grow withered, then I am ill; and if they die, that is a sign that I also am dead". That being done, he went away and came to an old man who took care of Ravàtovolòvoay's plantain-trees, and asked him, "What is it you take with you, when you go to visit your master?" The old man replied, "A few plantains, and some rice with honey, my lad". So in the morning — for he slept there that night — he plucked off the old man's hair from his head so that the whole skin from his body came away with it. Then Ibonia covered himself with it, while he fetched some plantains and prepared rice and honey to take to Ravàtovolòvoay. So he came presently to his village; and when the people there saw him they said, "The old man's come", for they did not know Ibonia, because he was covered with the old man's skin. Then he said, "I am come, children, to visit you". So they took the plantains and the rice which he had brought to the prince, for Ravàtovolòvoay was a prince. And they cooked rice for the old man (Ibonia) and gave it to him in the servants' plate, but he would not eat from that, but said, "Fetch me a plantain-leaf on which to eat. You know well enough how well my wife and I live, so why do you give me such a plate as that?" On the day following his arrival, it was announced that the chief would have sport with throwing at a mark with a cross-piece of wood, and so the old man went with the rest. When they came to the place where the mark was set up, the chief aimed at it, but not one of the people could hit it. Then said the old man, "Just give me a cord that I may catch hold of it". So they gave him one, and he was successful with the one the chief had missed. Then the chief said, "This is not the old man, but some one altogether different, so give me a spear and gun that I may attack him". But the old man said, "Why, who else is it but me, my son, for I am only showing the strength I used to possess?" So the chief let him off, and went on playing with the crosspiece of wood. And as they went on with the game the old man pressed in with the rest, but did not obtain what he aimed at, for the cross-piece went into the earth and brought up a hedgehog, and dipped into the water and brought out a crocodile. Then Ravàtovolòvoay said again, "Did I not tell you that this is not the old man, but some one else?" And again he sought to kill him; but the old man spoke as before, and so Ravàtovolòvoay again refrained.

One day following after that again, the chief's orders came saying, "Today we will try the tempers of the oxen, therefore make ropes to catch the stubborn ones". And when they began the game very many of the stronger oxen could not be caught. Then said the old man (Ibonia), "Just give me a rope". So they gave him one, and he caught the strong oxen and held them; and the people wondered when they saw it. And when the chief saw it, he said again, "This cannot be the old man, but some one else". But the people replied, "But who else can it be?" Then the old man answered again as he had done before, viz. that he was no one else, but was merely showing his strength. So the players dispersed.

And upon the following night, Ravàtovolòvoay went to his other wife; and upon that the old man (Ibonia) went to the house where Rampélasòamànanòro was, and said, "Let me lie here by the side of your feet". But she replied, "Why, what a wretch you must be, old man, to say such a thing to me, and speak of lying at my side". But when the people were fast asleep, Ibonia took off the skin of the old man with which he had covered himself, and there was a blaze of light in the house because of the shining of the skin of Ibonia. Then his wife knew him and said, "Is it you who have come?" "Yes", said he, "I have come to fetch you". So he bade the people go out of the house. And when they had gone out he bolted and barred the doors, and sat down to wait for the morning, that he might show some marvelous things to the people of the village. Then said Rampéla to Ibonia, "How shall we get from here?" He replied, "Don't be afraid, for we shall get out all right; but take heed what I say: do not speak to me or beckon to me, for if you do either they will kill me". So in the morning, when Ravàtovolòvoay awoke, he found that the door of the house where Rampela was was locked. Then he said to the people, "Isn't it just as I told you, that this is not the old man, but another person?" So he tried to break open the door; but the door became like a rock, and he could not force it. Then he set fire to the thatch of the roof; but it would not burn, but rather dropped down water. Then he dug round the foundation of the house; but that also became as rock.

And so, all his attempts being unavailing, at last Ibonia and Rampéla prepared to go out, and Ibonia caused a profound sleep to fall upon all the people outside the house, so that every one slept. Then he said to her, "Let us go, but do not speak to me or beckon to me". So they went out, and stepped over all the people who slept along the road they traveled. And when they came to the gateway, he beckoned to a lad and bade him awake the people. So the lad awoke and roused up all the people, and Ravàtovolòvoay as well. Then said he, "Bring quickly guns and spears; and come, let us pursue them!" So away they went, and shot at them with their guns; but when the smoke rolled away there was the pair going along without any harm. And so they went on without any mischance, until they came to the water-side; but when they got there the wife beckoned to him to ask him where to ford. But the moment she did so he was struck by a bullet, and fell back into the water and was dead. Then came up Ravàtovolòvoay to Rampéla and asked what she wished to do, to follow the living or the dead? She replied, "I will follow the living, sir", at the same time excusing herself to him.

And so Ibonia met his death, and his parents looked upon the arums and the plantain-tree which he had left with them as a token; and when they saw them dried up they lamented him, because the things were dead which he had given them as a sign about himself. However, his friends to whom he had made presents when he came from conquering Fòzanatokòndrilàhy had by no means forgotten him, and one day Joiner-together and his companions said to the Far-off-seer, "Look out for Ibonia, lest some harm should have befallen him". So he looked and said, "Ibonia is dead; and behold, yonder stream is carrying away his bones". Then said they all (Far-off-seer and Joiner-together and Life-giver) to Strong-swimmer: "Do you go and gather together those bones". So he went and gathered all the bones. Then Joiner-together united them, so that they all came together again, and Life-giver made them live. And they continued invoking blessings until flesh grew and a little breath came, and until he could eat a little rice, and so on, until at length he could eat as he had formerly been used to do. And when he was alive again he prepared to go and fetch his wife away from Ravàtovolòvoay. So he went off and when he came to his village there was the chief playing the game called *fanòrona* (something like "fox and geese") above the gateway. When he saw Ibonia he asked him, "Where are you going?" Said Ibonia, "To get my wife"; and, having thus answered each other, Ibonia struck him with the palm of his hand, and he became as grease in his hand; so Ibonia got everything that had belonged to Ravàtovolòvoay.

Motifs: D1610.2, Speaking tree. L215, Unpromising magic object chosen. D1501, Magic object assists woman in childbearing. T548.3, Magic elixir to produce a child. T61.5.3, Unborn children promised in marriage to each other. A511.1.2, Culture hero speaks before birth. A511.1.2.2, Culture hero in mother's womb indicates direction to be taken by her. A527.1, Culture hero precocious. T584.1, Birth through the mother's side. R11.1, Princess abducted by monster. F601, Persons of extraordinary powers. E761, Life token. K1941, Disguised flayer. D471.2.1, Transformation: house-door to stone. D1960, Magic sleep. C400, Speaking tabu. E127, Resuscitation by friends. R161.1, Lover rescues his lady from abductor.

Text 3. Merina tale collected 1875–1877. Summary by J. Richardson 102–104. Reprinted by Sibree "Malagasy Folk-Tales" 55–57.

A prince who lived in the center of the land had long been married, but no child had been born to him. He and his wife, anxious to become parents, sought out an old woman who could work an oracle, and she told them what to do to bring about the gratification of their wishes. They carried out her instructions by going into the forest and seeking out a suitable tree, and before it offered as a sacrifice a sheep and a goat. In due time a son was born in a most wonderful manner. They gave him the name of Bonia; and he appropriated to himself a razor his mother had swallowed, and used it ever afterwards as a wonder-working staff.

Another prince and his wife were also childless. They too sought out the old woman; and by carrying out her instructions obtained a daughter;

but she was a cripple and deformed. They called her Rakétabòlaména, or, as I will render it, "the Golden Beauty". This girl, ashamed of her lot, threatened to destroy herself if her father and mother would not station her on an island at some distance from their home. The poor father and mother were constrained sorrowfully to carry out her wish. To this lake the sons of several other princes resorted for wild-bird shooting, and were attracted to the house in which Golden Beauty dwelt by seeing her scarlet umbrella; but her servant so effectually hid herself and her mistress that the young fellows betook themselves off in fright. In the course of time Bonia came to the lake; and, having been foiled in his first attempt to find her, he made a second excursion; and his visit ended in his taking Beauty home as his wife, to the delight of all concerned.

Somewhere across the waters to the west there lived a monster of a man called Raivàto, who had the power of instantly transporting himself to any part of the world. Hearing of Bonia's beautiful wife, he determined to carry her off, and, taking advantage of Bonia's absence, he accomplished his purpose. Bonia set out after him; and in his travels he met with three men "in the shape of God", called, respectively, Prince Bone-setter, Prince Flesh-and-muscle-producer, and Prince Life-giver. He gave them food, and each adopted him as his child.

He again set out on his search. The sea was no obstacle to him, for he planted his staff in the ground, uttered his talismanic phrase, and walked over as on dry land. The crocodiles too came to his help, the eels and whales, &c. carried him; and when safely over, determined to test the reality of the powers of Bone-setter, Muscle-producer, and Life-giver, he uttered his talismanic phrase, thrust his staff into the ground, and lo! he dies, only to be brought to life again by their aid after three days.

Off he set again, and presently came up with Raivàto's gardener. His spear caused the man to shed his skin; and, having clothed himself in that, he gained admission into Raivàto's strongly fortified town, and revealed himself to his long-lost wife. Raivàto's gods informed him of Bonia's arrival and a terrible fight ensued; but Bonia's staff gave him the victory. He killed the monster and took his wife home; not only so, but, to the joy of all people, he restored to her lawful husband each and every woman whom Raivàto had carried off!

Such, leaving out the genealogy of each person concerned, the conversations, &c., all of which are given with the greatest minuteness, is the wonderful history of Bonia.

Motifs: D2161.3.11, Barrenness magically cured. T584.0.1, Childbirth assisted by magic. D1254, Magic staff. L112, Heroine of unpromising appearance. S325.0.1, Deformed child exposed. R161, Lover rescues his lady. R11.1, Princess (maiden) abducted by monster (ogre). F601, Extraordinary companions. K1941, Disguised flayer. D1317, Magic object warns of danger. D1400.1, Magic object conquers enemies. T100, Marriage.

Texts 4 and 5 are discussed in the "Texts" section of the introduction.

Text 6, "The king of the north and the king of the south". Merina tale collected 1907–1910 at Alasora, region of Antananarivo. Translated from Charles Renel 1:168–174. It is fairly close to Dahle's texts, featuring the barrenness and a *fanorona* game.

Andriambahoaka [Prince of the People] of the North and Andriambahoaka of the South, they say, each set out from his village. They happened to meet on a mountain where they both were expecting to rest. They greeted each other and talked together. Then they began to play *fanorona*. But neither could win, because each one was as strong as the other. So they agreed that if they had children of different sexes, they would marry them to each other. As a memorial to their meeting and what it led to, they erected a stone in that place.

After a time the wife of the lord of the North conceived, and the lord of the South heard about it. When she came to term, the queen of the North gave birth to a daughter, who was given the name Raboniamasoboniamanoro [Fair of Face, Charming]. When the woman was ready for marriage, her father let her know of the agreement he had made with the king of the South, and she promised to act accordingly. But she was very sad, because that king did not yet have a male child. Still, she said, "I will keep waiting, whether it's for a long time or a short time". Now one day, when she was walking out in the country some way from the village, Raivato (Stone Man) caught sight of her, they say. He was struck by her beauty and wanted to take her as his wife. He threw wild lemons to her, which she quickly picked up. Stone Man carried her off and took her far, far away, to an unknown country.

Some time after her disappearance, the wife of the lord of the South conceived. But, for a wonder, the child spoke while he was still in his mother's womb. He said, "Mama, mama! Swallow a little sharp knife for me!" The woman was very perplexed and consulted her husband. The lord of the South, they say, brought together his people to ask them if what the baby said should or should not be done. The people agreed to it. So the mother swallowed the knife in a banana, and the baby used it to open a passage for himself between her navel and the top of her womb. That was how he came out, and as soon as he was born, the slit closed up of itself. And they called the baby Ratombotombokatsorirangarangarana [Able-to-Withstand-False-Accusations].

He grew amazingly fast. At the end of his first week, he was as big as an eight-month-old; at the end of his second, like a boy of eight; at the end of his third week, he was stronger than the strongest man in the village. Soon he was looking to marry, and he asked his parents, "So where is my betrothed, the daughter of the King of the North?" His father explained to him that she had been carried off by Stone Man and that no one knew what had become of her. Ratombotombokatsorirangarangarana declared that he was going to set out and try to get her back. His parents tried in vain to discourage him from this crazy idea. They said to him that Stone Man was as hard as rock and as heavy as a boulder, and that it was as impossible to defeat him as for a river to pierce a mountain. But the young man persisted, and he asked his father and mother's blessing. Seeing they were getting nowhere, they allowed him to set out. Before leaving the village, he planted a tree to the west of his parents' house, and said to them: "So long as this tree is green and healthy, I will be all right. If it withers, it means I am in some danger; if it dries up, it means I shall be dead". Then he set out, carrying an axe, a spear and a rope.

When he reached the verge of the great forest, he cut one tree with his axe and said,

"Trees! trees! O trees of the forest

if I am princely by father and mother

let the trees of the forest separate

and open me an easy way!"

And all the trees divided before him. Next he arrived at a large sea. There was neither raft nor pirogue on the shore. He threw his spear into the water, saying,

"Water! water! O sacred water [= sea]

if I am princely by father and mother

let the sacred water separate

and open me an easy way!"

And the waters divided, and before him he saw completely dry ground to walk on.

Then he came to a high rock wall, which was impossible to cross. But he threw the rope, and with it he climbed right to the top. He walked a long time again, and arrived at the house of the keeper of Stone Man's fields. She was very old; her name was Ikonantitra (Old Lady). "Go away, go away, my child", she said. "Stone Man is harder than rock, heavier than a boulder! If you come close to him, he will kill you!" But Ratombotombokatsorirangarangarana asked her, "O, Old Lady: is he married?" "Yes, my child". "And what fruits do people usually present to him?" "What else but the fruits of that tree there?" the old woman answered, showing him a tall tree covered with blue fruit. The young man picked the fruits, then made his way towards Stone Man's house. But first he took the skin off Old Lady's face and covered his own face with it.

Stone Man ordered rice to be cooked for "her" to eat. The cooked rice was served in the earthenware bowl Old Lady usually used, but the bowl broke. Then it was put in a wooden bowl, which also broke; then in an iron plate, which also got broken. "What dish do you want to eat from, Old Lady?" "From the dish my son-in-law eats from", answered the sham old woman. "Get away, get away!" Stone Man replied. "You want to eat from the lord's plate — you ask for fruits that don't exist!" The young man left, and when he got back to the real Old Lady's house, he gave her back her skin.

Then he went to see Stone Man's fishermen. Just at that moment they were trying to raise their net, but in spite of all their efforts they could not manage it. One of them went to the lord's house and said, "My lord, a thing like this never happened in your grandfather's reign or your father's. We are trying in vain to raise our net, and we can't manage it". Then Stone Man tied up his loincloth, which went twelve times around his loins, and went to the waterside. But despite all his strength he too was unable to raise the net.

Now during his absence, Ratombotombokatsorirangarangarana had gone into Stone Man's wife's house. Charming-Fair-of-Face said to him, "Oh sir, leave at once! Why did you come here? If Stone Man saw you, he would certainly kill you".

"No, I am not leaving", the young man said. "For I am your husband and you are my wife". Then he told her his story and told her about the agreement that the King of the North and the King of the South had made. The young woman was very happy, but also she was very afraid, because she knew Stone Man's strength. And just then he came along. He rushed the door — Ratombotombokatsorirangarangarana did not have time to shut it completely — and he couldn't open it, though it stayed ajar. Then he set fire to the house. But the young woman cried out, "If I am princely by father and mother, let this house become a house of iron!" That happened.

Stone Man said to his rival, "Come on and fight. The woman will belong to the strongest one". The two men got ready for battle, and all the people put themselves in a circle around them to watch. [break in text]

"If I am princely by father and mother", said Ratombotombokatsorirangarangarana," may Stone Man be buried up to his chest!" And Stone Man was buried in the ground up to his chest. "If I am princely by father and mother", the young man said again, "let him be buried up to his neck!" And he was buried. "If I am princely by father and mother, let him be buried completely!" And he disappeared into the womb of the earth.

Meanwhile the tree the victor had planted had not withered, but kept growing, green and healthy. The man went back to his parents' house with his wife, and there were great celebrations.

Motifs: N1.3, Betting contest between two kings. T61.5.3, Unborn children promised in marriage to each other. M202, Fulfilling of bargain or promise. H316.1, Oranges (lemons) thrown to indicate princess's choice. R10.1, Princess (maiden) abducted. A511.1.2, Culture hero speaks before birth. T584.1, Birth through the mother's side. A511.4.1, Miraculous growth of culture hero. E761, Life token. D1273, Magic formula (charm). D1551, Waters magically divide and close. D1554, Magic forest opens and closes for hero to pass. D1675, Garden wall that cannot be overleapt. N825.3, Old woman helper. K1941, Disguised flayer. H71, Marks of royalty. H31, Recognition by unique ability. D522, Transformation through magic word. D470, Transformation: material of object changed. Q456, Burial alive as punishment. T100, Marriage.

Text 7, "Iafolavitra the adulterer". Tanala tale collected 1907–1910 in Ikongo region, Farafangana province. Translated from Renel 2:32–34.

Ifaranimahery (The-Ultimate-Strong), setting forth on an expedition, met a pregnant woman, they say, and said to her, "Mother, I am going to war. When you give birth, your son will be my brother, or your daughter will be my wife". The woman agreed to that, and after several months gave birth to a daughter. Soon Ultimate-Strong came to see her and claimed the child as his wife. Then he killed an ox, gave many clothes to his young wife, and again departed.

Meanwhile the woman grew up. When she was marriageable, since her husband had not yet come back, she said one day, "Mother, why doesn't someone ask for me in marriage?"

"Because you are married".

"Where is my husband?"

"He went to do some business years ago. The moment when you were born, that's when he was here".

"What's his name, mother?"

"His name is Ultimate-Strong".

The woman held on for a time, then got tired of vainly waiting for her husband. She ran away from her mother's house, because she really wanted to get married, and she made her way to the village of king *Indrianonibe* [Great Lord]. When he saw how beautiful she was, the king asked her to be his wife. "Gladly", she said. "I would be happy to marry you. Still I must confess to you, I am told that since I was born, I am the wife of Ultimate-Strong".

"Well then, in spite of my love for you, I ask you to excuse me, madame, but I do not want to take another man's wife".

She left there and soon arrived in the village of king *Iafolavitra* [Distant-Fire]. He was so struck with her beauty that he shouted, "I want you to be my wife".

"Me too, I am willing", the woman said. "But I must tell you that since I was born, I am the wife of Ultimate-Strong".

"Then where is your husband?"

"They tell me he's gone to do business in a faraway place, and that he left when I was still a baby".

"What the proverb says is right".

"What proverb?"

"You can't warm yourself by a distant fire".

The woman then agreed to become Distant-Fire's wife. Unfortunately, Ultimate-Strong found out that another man had taken his wife, and he prepared himself to win her back. Distant-Fire, for his part, called all his people together for war. The battle began soon, but all the men who threw spears at Ultimate-Strong fell dead as soon as he looked at them. The survivors ran away in a hurry. Distant-Fire was defeated and killed, and his kingdom passed into the hands of Ultimate-Strong, who got his wife back at the same time.

It's since then, they say, that no man may take away another man's wife.

Motifs: T61.5.1, Betrothal of hero to princess while both are still in cradle.T481.5, King takes subject's wife while her husband is sent away. T481, Adultery (equivalent here to R10.1, Princess abducted). F592, Man's glance kills.

Text 8, "Soavololonapanga" [Tender Fern]. Bara tale, written about 1934 by a schoolboy in Ranohira. Translated from Raymond Decary, *Contes et légendes du sud-ouest de Madagascar* 95–98.

There was a king, they say, called Razatovo (Mr. Young-Man), who married a very pretty woman named Soavololonapanga (Tender-Fern). Some time after their marriage, another king who had heard about her reputation for beauty (which they say was unique in the world) had a desire to get her for himself. Revato, the name of the second king (Stone-Man), sent a trusted man to steal Tender-Fern away so he could marry her. The messenger set out, but when he got near Young-Man's village he could not cross the river that separated the two kingdoms. Stone-Man then sent another man, who came back for the same reason. Finally a huge bird named *Vorombe-famaofao* (Kidnapper-Goose, i.e. Vulture) was sent by Stone-Man to get this desired woman. When he reached near Stone-Man's village, the bird saw Tender-Fern drawing water from the well. He seized her, the way a *papango* (kite) seizes a chick, and put her down in the yard of Stone-Man's palace. He was very glad to see his wish granted.

As for Young-Man, he waited a long time for his wife. That night he could not sleep, he was so upset about her disappearance. Finally he learned that a big bird took his wife to give her to Stone-Man, the king who lived on the other side of the river. Young-Man got ready to go and fetch his wife. He gathered several ropes and tied them into a long rope that would help him cross the river. When he reached the riverbank, this is what he did to get across. He tied one end of the rope to the foot of a big tree by the riverbank and tied the other end to his body. Then he plunged in, and because he was tied to the tree, the current could not carry him off, and he managed to cross the river in one piece.

When he got to Stone-Man's kingdom, Young-Man went near the village well to wait for Tender-Fern, because he meant to grab her if she happened to come to draw water there. When he got there, he climbed a big tree close to the well, the better to see people coming. He waited vainly for a long time; Tender-Fern still didn't come. Stone-Man did not want her to go and draw water herself, because he was afraid someone would come and carry her off as he had done himself. He sent one of the women of his court to go draw water for his new wife. When she got to the well, the woman drew water and filled her jug. When the jug was full, she looked at herself in the water. She saw Young-Man's face in the water and thought it was hers. She looked at herself and said, with that beautiful face she shouldn't carry the jug on her head. She broke her jug, because, said she, fine people like me would never carry a jug on their head. When she got to the village, she went to Stone-Man and told him that the jug got broken because the path to the well was slippery.

Stone-Man then sent a big woman past childbearing age to fetch water, but she did the same as the other one when she saw Young-Man's face in the water, thinking it was her own face. Finally he sent an old woman to take their place.

When she got to the well, she began to draw water, but imagine her surprise when she saw a young face sparkling in the water of the well. She understood that it was someone in the tree reflected in the water, and that the women didn't know that, and that's why they broke their jugs. She looked up into the tree and saw Young-Man, who was quietly coming down. He asked the old woman who she was drawing water for. The old woman answered that it was for Stone-Man's new wife. Then Young-Man pulled on her hair, and her skin came off in one piece. He took the old woman's skin and went up to the village, disguised as an old woman who walked painfully.

When he came before the king's palace, he asked where to put the water. The king ordered it put into Tender-Fern's house, which he pointed to with his finger. The false old woman asked too if she could spend the night in Tender-Fern's house, because she was very cold and tired and could not go home. Stone-Man granted her this favor, for he didn't recognize Young-Man in the disguise of an old woman.

When everyone was quietly asleep, Young-Man took off the old woman's skin that was covering his body and lit the fire to show himself to his wife. Tender-Fern was surprised to see Young-Man, who she thought all the time was an old woman. Just then Young-Man took his wife and went back to his village. The next day Stone-Man was disagreeably surprised at his wife's disappearance, and understood too late that that was a false old

He told him to call all his servants and he would undertake to cure him. When they had all come together, he ordered them to go look for stones as big as someone's mouth. When he had them, the clever little fellow took one and heated it in the fire. Then he took it out and had his adoptive father, who was over-credulous, swallow it. He died. Then he called for his wife Kitanandrofamazava, and they both became owners of Great-Stone-Man's riches.

Motifs: T513.1.1, Impregnation by magician's power. T548.2, Magic rites for obtaining a child. T575.1, Child speaks in mother's womb. T584.1, Birth through mother's side. T585.5.1, Child born with hairy mane. K2211.1, Treacherous brother-in-law. K2214.3.1, Treacherous foster son. K1955, Sham physician. K951.1, Murder by throwing hot stones in the mouth.

Text 14, "The story of Ravato-Rabonia". Sakalava, 1970s. Translated from the French translation by Suzanne Chazan-Gillig 159–163.

Once there was a polygamous prince. His first wife (the older, the first one the prince married, the one recognized as the real wife, who receives all the rights accorded to the wife so named), gave birth to a son called Ravato. When he was old enough to marry, his father offered him a girl called Soamananoro, and he married her. The prince said then that they could not live together in the palace with him; that was the tradition, lest there be disagreements between father and son. The young couple settled on the other side of the sea (on the other bank).

The second wife, shortly after, gave birth to Rabonia. Rabonia grew in age and wisdom. He was given (his mother gave him) Rasihotse as a wife.

"I won't have that woman," he said, "because she has a big mouth. I don't like her."

"Whom would you like, then?" said his mother.

"Anyway I don't like that one!" he answered.

His mother offered him Rakelitamana. She attracted him, but he found her legs too small. "What do you want, then?" his mother repeated.

"The one I love is Soamananoro," he said.

"But Soamananoro is Ravato's wife. They live on the other side," his mother said.

"No, mama," he said, "I am going for Soamananoro."

"The ground has steep cracks, the mosses are like guineafowl, their thorns are like the horns of three castrated oxen."

"Yes," said Rabonia, "but as I am resolved to marry, I will go anyway."

Rabonia went to see an *ombiasa* [diviner]. He went hunting; that was an amusement of kings in those days. A hundred men went with him. While Rabonia was lying in the shade, his men went to take game, good game for king Rabonia's meal. Rabonia went walking and met Konantitse. "How are you, Konantitse? I come to see you because I need an *ody*," said Rabonia.

"What kind of *ody* do you want?"

"Everything you are willing to give me."

"I have *mantaloha.*"

"All right, I'll take that one, I'll buy it," said Rabonia. He took the *ody* and asked Konantitse how to use it.

"This is a speaking *ody*," Konantitse said. "The only thing forbidden to it is the mouth. Above all don't lie down at the mouth of a river or beside water."

Rabonia took it with him and called together all his people (his whole retinue), and they left. At home he told his mother he was leaving.

"Oh, you are leaving?" his mother said.

"Yes," he said.

And on the day he was going to battle, he called together three hundred men, two hundred castrated oxen. They set out to go across the sea. "*Mantaloha*," he said, "what do we do to cross this whole sea?" Where they passed, all the places they trod dried up, and the places they did not pass were entirely covered in water. They went on their way, always carrying their *ody* with them, and their cattle with them. They went on. When Rabonia learned (he did not believe his ears) that mosquitoes were stinging the oxen and making them run, he asked advice from the *mantaloha*: "What must we do against the mosquitoes?"

"Spread ashes on them," it said.

No sooner said than done, and the mosquitoes disappeared.

The king and his retinue met with thorns, farther on, and again Rabonia asked advice of the *mantaloha,* which told them to keep going forward, because, it said, nothing was there. When they got to the other side of the sea, Rabonia told the three hundred men with him, and the two hundred oxen, to stay there waiting for him to come back after he took care of Ravato. "Eat everything you can," he said. "While I'm away you can go as far as Lavasomotse to get food." Then Rabonia set out with his *mantaloha*, asking it, "*mantaloha*, where is Ravato's well?"

"Why, it's over there," the *mantaloha* said. They set out, and Rabonia reached Ravato's well. "Is this really Ravato's well?" Rabonia asked. "Yes," the *mantaloha* said.

Rabonia climbed a tree. Then Ravato's slaves came to fetch water, arriving with their gourds to fetch water. "Oh, how beautiful I am," said every one of them, seeing Rabonia's face reflected in the water of the well; the well was golden. They broke their gourds. The ones left in the village asked why. "Well, because we've become beautiful now, we let everything drop."

Konantitse, who lived in that village, asked them why they acted like that, and decided to go there himself to draw water. He scolded them for what they'd done: "What are we going to do now, we can't drink water." Konantitse went to draw water, carrying his stick; he reached the well. "A flower from beyond the sea has come here," he said. Rabonia came down from the tree, seized Konantitse, spun him around, his whole body came apart. He set Konantitse's skin out to dry. When it was dry, Rabonia grabbed it and set out for Ravato's country. First he asked the *mantaloha* how to find a house they could stay in. The *mantaloha* promised to take him to Konantitse's house. Rabonia wanted to take Soamananoro as his wife, that's why he crossed all the regions between them.

So Rabonia was living in Konantitse's house, he made his meal, he ate there. Prince Ravato wanted to castrate his oxen, so he called all his people together for the next day, and people had to come from all directions. Rabonia, disguised as Konantitse, asked the prince's permission to be present for this event, as a memory of his childhood. Prince Ravato saw no problem with that. Rabonia said to the *mantaloha*, "How can we hold on to these oxen?"

"Don't worry," said the *mantaloha*, "they won't hurt us."

Rabonia took hold of one big ox, it was castrated right away. Ravota was astounded, and said to himself that wasn't Konantitse but somebody else. "You want to kill me," said Konantitse. "Why don't you believe me?"

"I'll leave you alone."

He got up to go back to his house. Ravato announced that next day, there would be a *kirijy* contest (a tin hoop rolled forward with a bamboo stick; boys compete to catch it). The people came together at the beginning of the day. They divided up into two teams, ten men on each side. Rabonia looked on, under Konantitse's skin; the *mantaloha* was with him. The game began, they launched a hoop, it was caught by the other side, and so on. "This game makes me think of my childhood," said Konantitse (really Rabonia).

"What was that?" Ravato said.

"I am thinking of my games of old times," Konantitse answered. "May I play?"

"Yes," said Ravato.

Konantitse joined the game, leaning on his stick. Rabonia caught the hoop every time it was thrown at him, while normally, ten men would have had their legs broken. Ravato said that the winner was not Konantitse and set out hunting.

Rabonia took advantage of this well-timed moment to go up to Ravato's wife and say, "Are you really Soamananoro?"

"Yes, I am," said the woman.

"I've come to get you and take you home," Rabonia said. "Ravato and I are the sons of two sisters (the king's wives), he's the son of the first wife, I'm the son of the second. Come, let's go back. Will you go back with me?"

"Yes," said Soamananoro, "we can go first thing in the morning."

Ravato was still out hunting, night began to fall, he wasn't too far away to get back, for there were a lot of boars, having eaten all he'd found in the forest. Rabonia and Soamananoro set forth the day Ravato came back. At the beginning of the day, Rabonia consulted the *mantaloha*: "What'll we say, as we are bringing Ravato's wife with us?"

"No problem," said the *mantaloha*. "Let's go!" They started out. When they reached the well, Rabonia put down the skin on the old man's lifeless body. Rabonia wondered what to do with this person they'd killed. The *mantaloha* reassured him and told him just to put the skin down on the dead body, and it came back to life. They went on, went on, and reached the place where the three hundred men were waiting. They asked them how things had gone. Rabonia declared that he had Soamananoro, and that before they left, they would wait there for Ravato.

Ravato reached home after Rabonia left with Soamananoro. The *masondrano* [king's minister] came to welcome him, and told him Rabonia had taken his wife away, with her consent. "I knew it (I foresaw it)," said Ravato.

The horn was blown, and it was announced that the people were distressed because Rabonia had taken away the prince's wife. "Let us go pursue them," the voice went on. Everyone agreed. They set out, and saw that Rabina was out on the sea, but the *mantaloha* had transformed that place into dry land; Ravato and his retinue got there. Rabonia incited Ravato to battle, "for if I have touched someone's property," he said, "it's because I am ready to do battle. I am a Man."

"We won't fight some place else, but here, in front of our men." Ravato's and Rabonia's men fought with swords, axes, machetes (big, sharp knives). Not one of the men was left.

"So let's fight, the two of us," said Ravato.

"What do you think about a battle with Ravato?" Rabonia said to the *mantaloha*.

"Go ahead," the *mantaloha* answered. "He won't manage to kill us. Fasten me under your clothes." Rabonia put on his *sadia* [waist-cloth] and fastened the *mantaloha* underneath. Then the two princes approached each other, not to fight with swords but to wrestle. Ravato grabbed Rabonia's whole body, and Rabonia sank into the ground, then Rabonia got back up and a well was formed there where he passed, a well that spouted up to high ground. Rabonia was astounded: "That does it," he said. He took Ravato and threw him to the ground, a marsh sprang up. Ravato came out of that, expressing his discontent: "I am your elder, and you are thrownig me down like this?!" The battle began again. Ravato took Rabonia, put him under water, and he came out but a big hole formed there, of the water springing out of the place where it was gushing.

"I am wrong," said Rabonia. "What do you say, *mantaloha*?"

"Attack, we're going to beat him," it said.

Rabonia took Ravato; he fell back, he died.

"We're going to leave," said Rabonia, "for Ravato has reached his destination (at home)." "Which way do we go?" Rabonia asked the *mantaloha*.

"That way. We'll go by the road we came on," said the *mantaloha*. So Rabonia brought Soamananoro home. She was a very pretty woman. They reached the other side of the sea. Rabonia reigned, having got such a pretty wife. Ravato angry followed them from under ground. He tried to raise his head. That was the origin of all those blocks of stone along the bank on this side, on the red earth there. The head left traces on the surface. That's why there are blocks of stone here and there; Ravato wanted to come out of his hole, but couldn't. He was a man turned to stone, that's what gave him the name Ravato.

I am not responsible. Not my story, but from the ancestors who told lies. (In short, it's only a story.)

Motifs: P251.5, Two brothers. K1371, Bride-stealing. D1312, Magic object gives advice. K1941, Disguised flayer dresses in skin of his victim.

Works Cited

Abrams, M. H., gen. ed., *The Norton Anthology of English Literature, Volume 2*, Sixth edition (New York: W. W. Norton, 1993).

Afanasiev, Alexander Nikolaevich, *Russian Folk-tales* (New York: Funk and Wagnalls, 1969).

African Folklore, An Encyclopedia, see Peek.

Almereyda, Michael, film adaptation of *Hamlet* by William Shakespeare (2000).

Baron, Robert, and Ana C. Cara, eds., *Creolization as Cultural Creativity* (Jackson, MS: University Press of Mississippi, 2011).

Barthes, Roland, 'The Death of the Author', in *The Rustle of Language*, trans. Richard Howard (New York: Hill and Wang, 1986), pp. 49–55.

Bascom, William, 'Cinderella in Africa', *Journal of the Folklore Institute* 9, no. 1 (1972), 54–69.

—, 'The Forms of Folklore: Prose Narratives', in *Sacred Narrative: Readings in the Theory of Myth*, ed. Alan Dundes (Berkeley and Los Angeles, CA: University of California Press, 1984), pp. 5–29.

—, 'Four Functions of Folklore', in *The Study of Folklore*, ed. Alan Dundes (Englewood Cliffs, N.J.: Prentice-Hall, 1965), pp. 279–298.

Bauman, Richard, 'The Field Study of Folklore in Context', in *Handbook of American Folklore*, ed. Richard M. Dorson (Bloomington, IN: Indiana University Press, 1983), pp. 362–367.

—, 'Performance', in *International Encyclopedia of Communications*, ed. Erik Barnouw (New York: Oxford University Press, 1989), vol. 3, pp. 262–266.

—, *Story, Performance and Event: Contextual Studies of Oral Narrative* (Cambridge: Cambridge University Press, 1986).

—, *Verbal Art as Performance* (Prospect Heights, IL: Waveland Press, 1977).

Beaujard, Philippe, *Mythe et société à Madagascar (Tanala de l'Ikongo): le chasseur d'oiseaux et la princesse du ciel* (Paris: L'Harmattan, 1991).

Becker, R., translator, *Conte d'Ibonia*, Mémoires de l'Académie Malgache (Antananarivo: Imprimerie Moderne de l'Émyrne, Pitot de la Beaujardière, 1939).

Belcher, Stephen, *Epic Traditions of Africa* (Bloomington, IN: Indiana University Press, 1999).

Ben-Amos, Dan, '"Context" in Context', *Western Folklore* 52 (1993), 209–226.

—, 'Toward a Definition of Folklore in Context', *Journal of American Folklore* 84, no. 331 (January–March 1971), 3–15.

Bendix, Regina, *In Search of Authenticity: The Formation of Folklore Studies* (Madison, WI: University of Wisconsin Press, 1997).

Bhabha, Homi K., *The Location of Culture* (London: Routledge, 1994).

Biebuyck, Daniel, 'The African Heroic Epic', in *Heroic Epic and Saga: An Introduction to the World's Great Folk Epics*, ed. Felix J. Oinas (Bloomington, IN: Indiana University Press, 1978), pp. 336–367.

—, *Hero and Chief: Epic Literature from the Banyanga, Zaïre Republic* (Berkeley and Los Angeles, CA: University of California Press, 1978).

Birkeli, Émile, 'Folklore sakalava recueilli dans la région de Morondava', *Bulletin de l'Académie Malgache* n. s. 6 (1922–1923), 185–417.

Blackburn, Stuart H., and A. K. Ramanujan, *Another Harmony: New Essays on the Folklore of India* (Berkeley and Los Angeles, CA: University of California Press, 1986).

Bloch, Maurice, *From Blessing to Violence: History and Ideology in the Circumcision Ritual of the Merina of Madagascar* (Cambridge: Cambridge University Press, 1986).

—, *Placing the Dead: Tombs, Ancestral Villages and Kinship Organisation Among the Merina of Madagascar* (London: Seminar Press, 1971).

—, *Ritual, History and Power: Selected Papers in Anthropology* (London: Athlone Press, 1989).

Boas, Franz, *The Mind of Primitive Man* (New York: Macmillan, 1938).

Bouillon, Antoine, *Madagascar, le colonisé et son "âme": essai sur le discourse psychologique colonial* (Paris: L'Harmattan, 1981).

Briggs, Charles L., 'Metadiscursive Practices and Scholarly Authority in Folkloristics', *Journal of American Folklore* 106, no. 422 (Fall 1993), 387–434.

Brown, Mervyn, *Madagascar Rediscovered: A History from Early Times to Independence* (Hamden, CN: Archon Books, 1979).

Calame-Griaule, Geneviève, 'L'art de la parole dans la culture africaine', *Présence Africaine* 47, 2ème trimestre (1963), 73–91.

Callet, R. P., *Tantaran'ny andriana* (originally *Tantara ny andriana eto Madagascar*), trans. G.-S. Chapus and E. Ratsimba (Antananarivo: Académie Malgache, 1958).

Carver, Raymond, *What We Talk About When We Talk About Love: Stories* (New York: Vintage Books, 1989).

Chapus, Georges-Sully, *Les imériniens dans les "contes des anciens"* (Montpellier: Imprimerie Causse, Graille et Castelnau, 1930).

Chatelain, Héli, *Folk-Tales of Angola. Fifty Tales, with Ki-Mbundu Text, Literal English Translation, Introduction, and Notes. Collected and Edited*, Memoirs of the American Folk-lore Society, 1 (Boston: Houghton Mifflin, 1894).

Chazan-Gillig, Suzanne, *La société sakalave: le menabe dans la construction nationale malgache (1947–1972)* (Paris: Éditions de l'ORSTOM, Éditions Karthala, 1991).

Clements, William M., ed., *The Greenwood Encyclopedia of World Folklore and Folklife*, 4 vols. (Westport, CT: Greenwood Press, 2006).

Cole, Jennifer, *Forget Colonialism?: Sacrifice and the Art of Memory in Madagascar* (Berkeley, CA: University of California Press, 2001).

Cousins, W. E., *Madagascar of Today* (London: The Religious Tract Society, 1895).

Dahle, Lars, *Specimens of Malagasy Folk-Lore* (Antananarivo: A. Kingdon, 1877).

— and rev. John Sims, *Anganon'ny Ntaolo: tantara mampiseho ny fomban-drazana sy ny finoana sasany nananany* (Antananarivo: Trano Printy Loterana, 1971).

— and rev. John Sims, *Contes des aieux malgaches (Anganon'ny Ntaolo)*, trans. Denise Dorian and Louis Molet, Études Océan Indien, 14 (Paris: Institut des Langues et Civilisations Orientales, 1992).

Dandouau, André, *Contes populaires des sakalava et des tsimihety de la région d'Analalava*, Publications de la Faculté des Lettres d'Alger, 58 (Algiers: Jules Carbonel, 1922).

Decary, Raymond, *Contes et légendes du sud-ouest de Madagascar* (Paris: G.-P. Maisonneuve et Larose, 1964).

—, *Moeurs et coutumes des malgaches* (Paris: Payot, 1951).

Delivré, Alain, *L'histoire des rois d'Imerina: interprétation d'une tradition orale* (Paris: Klincksieck, 1974).

Deschamps, Hubert, *Histoire de Madagascar,* fourth edition (Paris: Berger-Levrault, 1972).

Domenichini-Ramiaramanana, Bakoly, 'Les traductions poétiques des hainteny', in *Colloque sur la traduction poétique* (Paris: Gallimard, 1978), pp. 103–150.

Dorson, Richard M., *American Folklore*, The Chicago History of American Civilization (Chicago, IL: University of Chicago Press, 1959).

—, *The British Folklorists, A History* (Chicago, IL: University of Chicago Press, 1968).

—, 'The Eclipse of Solar Mythology', in *The Study of Folklore*, ed. Alan Dundes (Englewood Cliffs, N.J.: Prentice-Hall, 1965), pp. 57–83.

Dumézil, Georges, *The Destiny of a King,* trans. Alf Hiltebeitel (Chicago, IL: University of Chicago Press, 1973).

—, *The Destiny of the Warrior*, trans. Alf Hiltebeitel (Chicago, IL: University of Chicago Press, 1970).

—, *The Plight of a Sorcerer*, trans. David Weeks et al. (Berkeley, CA: University of California Press, 1986).

Dundes, Alan, ed., *The Study of Folklore* (Englewood Cliffs, N.J.: Prentice-Hall, 1965).

—, 'Texture, Text and Context', *Southern Folklore Quarterly* 28 (1964), 251–265.

Eagleton, Terry, *Criticism and Ideology: A Study in Marxist Literary Theory* (London: Verso Editions, 1978).

Edmonson, Munro S., *Lore: An Introduction to the Science of Folklore and Literature* (New York: Holt, Rinehart and Winston, 1971).

Emoff, Ron, *Recollecting from the Past: Musical Practice and Spirit Possession on the East Coast of Madagascar* (Middletown, CT: Wesleyan University Press, 2002).

Étiemble, René, 'Épopée', in *Encyclopedia Universalis* (Paris: Encyclopedia Universalis, 1968), vol. 6, pp. 375–377.

Fanony, Fulgence, *L'oiseau grand-tison et autres contes des betsimisaraka du nord (Madagascar)* (Paris: L'Harmattan, 2001).

Faublée, Jacques, *Récits bara* (Paris: Institut d'Ethnologie, Musée de l'Homme, 1947).

Feeley-Harnik, Gillian, *A Green Estate: Restoring Independence in Madagascar* (Washington D.C.: Smithsonian Institution Press, 1991).

Fernandez, James W., *Persuasions and Performances: The Play of Tropes in Culture* (Bloomington, IN: Indiana University Press, 1986).

Ferrand, Gabriel, *Contes populaires malgaches* (Paris: Ernest Leroux, 1893).

Flacourt, Étienne de, *Histoire de la Grande Isle Madagascar* (Paris: Gervais Clouzier, 1661).

Finnegan, Ruth, *Oral Literature in Africa* (Oxford: Clarendon Press, 1970). Revised edition (Cambridge: Open Book Publishers, 2012) DOI: 10.11647/OBP.0025.

Flannagan, Roy, ed., *The Riverside Milton* (Boston: Houghton Mifflin, 1998).

Fontenrose, Joseph, *Python: A Study of Delphic Myth and its Origins* (Berkeley, CA: University of California Press, 1959).

Fox, Leonard, *Hainteny: The Traditional Poetry of Madagascar* (Lewisburg, PA: Bucknell University Press, 1990).

Gates, Henry Louis, *The Signifying Monkey: A Theory of Afro-American Literary Criticism* (New York: Oxford University Press, 1988).

Georges, Robert A., 'Toward an Understanding of Storytelling Events', *Journal of American Folklore* 82 (1969), 313–328.

Glassie, Henry, *Passing the Time in Ballymenone: Culture and History of an Ulster Community* (Philadelphia, PA: University of Pennsylvania Press, 1982).

Goffman, Erving, *Forms of Talk*, University of Pennsylvania Publications in Conduct and Communication (Philadelphia, PA: University of Pennsylvania Press, 1981).

—, *Frame Analysis: An Essay on the Organization of Experience* (Harmondsworth: Penguin Books, 1975).

—, *Interaction Ritual: Essays on Face-to-Face Behavior* (Garden City, NY: Doubleday, 1967).

Gow, Bonar A., *Madagascar and the Protestant Impact: The Work of the British Missions, 1818–1895* (London: Longman, 1979).

Greenwood Encyclopedia, see Clements.

Grimm, Jakob, and Wilhelm Grimm, *The Complete Fairy Tales of the Brothers Grimm*, trans. Jack Zipes (New York: Bantam Books, 1992).

Haring, Lee, 'Malagasy Riddling', *Journal of American Folklore* 98 (1985), 163–190.

—, *Malagasy Tale Index*, FF Communications no. 231 (Helsinki: Suomalainen Tiedeakatemia, 1982).

—, *Verbal Arts in Madagascar: Performance in Historical Perspective* (Philadelphia, PA: University of Pennsylvania Press, 1992).

Hurston, Zora Neale, *Mules and Men* (Philadelphia, PA: J. B. Lippincott, 1935).

Hymes, Dell, 'Introduction: Toward Ethnographies of Communication', *American Anthropologist* 66, no. 6, part 2 (1964), 1–34.

—, *Now I Know Only So Far: Essays in Ethnopoetics* (Lincoln, NE: University of Nebraska Press, 2003).

Jakobson, Roman, 'Two Aspects of Language and Two Types of Aphasic Disturbances', in *Fundamentals of Language,* Roman Jakobson and Morris Halle, second edition. (The Hague: Mouton, 1971), pp. 67–96.

Johnson, John William, 'Yes, Virginia, There Is an Epic in Africa', *Research in African Literatures* 11 (1980), 306–326.

—, Thomas A. Hale and Stephen Belcher, eds., *Oral Epics from Africa: Vibrant Voices from a Vast Continent* (Bloomington, IN: Indiana University Press, 1997).

Kent, Raymond K., *Early Kingdoms in Madagascar, 1500–1700* (New York: Holt, Rinehart and Winston, 1970).

Kirshenblatt-Gimblett, Barbara, 'A Parable in Context: A Social Interactional Analysis of Storytelling Performance', in *Folklore: Performance and Communication,* ed. Dan Ben-Amos and Kenneth S. Goldstein (The Hague: Mouton, 1974), pp. 105–130.

Kluckhohn, Clyde, 'Recurrent Themes in Myth and Mythmaking', in *The Study of Folklore,* ed. Alan Dundes (Englewood Cliffs, N.J.: Prentice-Hall, 1965), pp. 158–168.

Kottak, Conrad Phillip, *The Past in the Present: History, Ecology, and Cultural Variation in Highland Madagascar* (Ann Arbor, MI: University of Michigan Press, 1980).

Lakoff, George, and Mark Johnson, *Metaphors We Live By* (Chicago, IL: University of Chicago Press, 2003).

Lanting, Frans, *Madagascar, A World Out of Time* (New York: Aperture, 1990).

Lévy-Bruhl, Lucien, *How Natives Think* (London: George Allen & Unwin, 1926).

Lomax, Alan, *Folk Song Style and Culture* (Washington D.C.: American Association for the Advancement of Science, 1968).

Lord, Albert, *The Singer of Tales* (Cambridge, MA: Harvard University Press, 1960).

Mack, John, *Madagascar, Island of the Ancestors* (London: British Museum Publications, 1986).

Mandihitsy, C., J.-F. Rabedimy, and Velonandro [pseudonym for Noël J. Gueunier], *Tsimamangafaiahy, ou l'homme qui s'est circoncis lui-même, et autres récits. Contes malgaches en dialecte masikoro* (Toliara, Madagascar: Établissement de l'enseignement supérieur des lettres, 1989).

Marzolph, Ulrich, 'Folktale, "Tale Type"', in *South Asian Folklore, An Encyclopedia,* ed. Peter Claus, Sarah Diamond and Margaret A. Mills (New York: Routledge, 2003), pp. 220–222.

Michel, Louis, *Moeurs et coutumes des bara,* Mémoires de l'Académie Malgache (Antananarivo: Institut Scientifique de Madagascar, 1957).

Michel-Andrianarahinjaka, Lucien X., 'De l'origine des princes, d'après les contes malgaches', *Bulletin de l'Académie Malgache* 43 (1965), 16–19.

—, *Le système littéraire betsileo* (Fianarantsoa: Éditions Ambozontany, 1986).

Musée d'Ethnographie de Neuchâtel, *Malgache, Qui es-Tu?* (Neuchâtel: Musée d'Ethnographie de Neuchâtel, 1973).

Noiret, François, *Le mythe d'Ibonia* (Antananarivo: Foi et Justice, 1993).

—, Review of *Ibonia, Epic of Madagascar* by Lee Haring, *Cahiers de Littérature Orale* 36 (1995), 163–166.

Okpewho, Isidore, *The Epic in Africa* (New York: Columbia University Press, 1979).

Ottino, Paul, 'Ancient Malagasy Dynastic Succession: The Merina Example', *History in Africa* 10 (1983), 247–292.

—, 'Les andriambahoaka malgaches et l'héritage indonésien', in *Les souverains de Madagascar*, ed. Françoise Raison-Jourde (Paris: Karthala, 1983), pp. 71–96.

—, *L'étrangère intime: essai d'anthropologie de la civilisation de l'ancien Madagascar* (Paris: Éditions des Archives Contemporaines, 1986).

—, 'Myth and History: The Malagasy Andriambahoaka and the Indonesian Legacy', *History in Africa* 9 (1983), 221–250.

—, 'The Mythology of the Highlands of Madagascar and the Political Cycle of the Andriambahoaka', in *Mythologies: A Restructured Translation of Dictionnaire des mythologies et des religions des sociétés traditionnelles et du monde antique*, ed. Yves Bonnefoy and Wendy Doniger (Chicago, IL: University of Chicago Press, 1991), vol. 2, pp. 961–976.

—, 'Un procédé littéraire malayo-polynésien: de l'ambigüité à la plurisignification', *L'Homme* 6, no. 4 (October–December 1966), 5–34.

Palmenfelt, Ulf, 'On the Understanding of Folk Legends', in *Telling Reality: Folklore Studies in Memory of Bengt Holbek*, ed. Michael Chesnutt (Copenhagen: Nordic Institute of Folklore, 1993), pp. 143–167.

Paulhan, Jean, *Les hain-teny merinas, poésies populaires malgaches* (Paris: P. Geuthner, 1913).

—, *Les hain-tenys* (Paris: Gallimard, 1960).

Peek, Philip M., and Kwesi Yankah, eds., *African Folklore, An Encyclopedia* (New York: Routledge, 2004).

Pound, Ezra, *Selected Poems of Ezra Pound* (Norfolk, CN: New Directions, 1957).

Propp, V., *Morphology of the Folktale*, trans. Laurence Scott, second edition (Austin, TX: University of Texas Press, 1968).

—, *Theory and History of Folklore*, ed. Anatoly Liberman (Minneapolis, MN: University of Minnesota Press, 1984).

Puhvel, Jaan, *Comparative Mythology* (Baltimore, MD: Johns Hopkins University Press, 1987).

Raglan, Lord, *The Hero: A Study in Tradition, Myth, and Drama* (New York: Vintage Books, 1956).

Raison-Jourde, Françoise, 'Introduction', in *Les souverains de Madagascar: l'histoire royale et ses résurgences contemporaines*, ed. Françoise Raison-Jourde (Paris: Karthala, 1983).

Ramamonjisoa, Suzy, Maurice Schrive, Solo Raharijanahary, and Velonandro [pseudonym for Noël J. Gueunier], *Femmes et monstres 1: tradition orale malgache* (Paris: EDICEF, 1981).

Renel, Charles, *Contes de Madagascar* (Paris: Ernest Leroux, 1910).

Richardson, John, 'Iboniamasiboniamanoro', *Antananarivo Annual* 3 (1877), 102–104. Reprinted by James Sibree, Jr., *Folk-lore Journal* 2 (1884), 55–57.

—, 'More Folk-Lore', *Antananarivo Annual* 4 (1878), 44–53.

Ruud, Jørgen, *Taboo: A Study of Malagasy Customs and Beliefs* (Oslo: Oslo University Press, 1960).

Said, Edward W., 'Yeats and Decolonisation', in *Nationalism, Colonialism, and Literature* (Minneapolis, MN: University of Minnesota Press, 1990), pp. 69–95.

Scheub, Harold, 'A Review of African Oral Traditions and Literature', *African Studies Review* 28 (1985), 1–72.

Seydou, Christiane, 'The African Epic: A Means for Defining the Genre', *Folklore Forum* 16, no. 1 (1983), 47–68.

Sibree, James, Jr., 'Malagasy Folk-Tales', *Folk-Lore Journal* 2 (1884), 45–57.

—, 'The Oratory, Songs, Legends, and Folk-Tales of the Malagasy', *Folk-Lore Journal* 1 (1883), 305–316.

— and John Richardson, *Folk-Lore and Folk-Tales of Madagascar* (Tananarive: London Missionary Society Press, 1886).

Thompson, Stith, *Motif-Index of Folk-Literature: A Classification of Narrative Elements in Folktales, Ballads, Myths, Fables, Mediaeval Romances, Exempla, Fabliaux, Jest-Books, and Local Legends* (Bloomington, IN: Indiana University Press, 1955–1958).

Uther, Hans-Jörg, *The Types of International Folktales: A Classification and Bibliography*, FF Communications no. 284, 3 vols. (Helsinki: Suomalainen Tiedeakatemia, 2004).

Veyrières, P. Paul, *Le livre de la sagesse malgache* (Paris: Éditions maritimes et d'outre-mer, 1967).

West, M. L., *Indo-European Poetry and Myth* (Oxford: Oxford University Press, 2007).

Wilson, William A., *Folklore and Nationalism in Modern Finland* (Bloomington, IN: Indiana University Press, 1976).

Index

This book does not end here...

At Open Book Publishers, we are changing the nature of the traditional academic book. The title you have just read will not be left on a library shelf, but will be accessed online by hundreds of readers each month across the globe. We make all our books free to read online so that students, researchers and members of the public who can't afford a printed edition can still have access to the same ideas as you. Our digital publishing model also allows us to produce online supplementary material, including extra chapters, reviews, links and other digital resources. Find *How to Read a Folktale* on our website to access its online extras. Please check this page regularly for ongoing updates, and join the conversation by leaving your own comments:

http://www.openbookpublishers.com/isbn/9781909254053

If you enjoyed this book, and feel that research like this should be available to all readers, regardless of their income, please think about donating to us. Our company is run entirely by academics, and our publishing decisions are based on intellectual merit and public value rather than on commercial viability. We do not operate for profit and all donations, as with all other revenue we generate, will be used to finance new Open Access publications. For further information about what we do, how to donate to OBP, additional digital material related to our titles or to order our books, please visit our website: www.openbookpublishers.com

The World Oral Literature Project is an urgent global initiative to document and disseminate endangered oral literatures before they disappear without record. Our website houses collections of recordings of oral literature, free-to-download publications of documentation theory and practice, and links to resources and funding for oral tradition fieldwork and archiving: www.oralliterature.org

In partnership with Open Book Publishers, the World Oral Literature Project has launched a book series on oral literature. The series preserves and promotes the oral literatures of indigenous people by publishing materials on endangered traditions in innovative ways.

OpenBook Publishers

Knowledge is for sharing

www.ingramcontent.com/pod-product-compliance
Lightning Source LLC
Chambersburg PA
CBHW070911030726
47504CB00005B/1547